Blowback

Other Books by Emmy Curtis

Pushing the Limit

Over the Line

Dangerous Territory (novella)

Blowback

EMMY CURTIS

New York

Forever Yours
Hachette Book Group
1290 Avenue of the Americas
New York, NY 10104

www.HachetteBookGroup.com

Printed in the United States of America

First trade POD edition: November 2015

10 9 8 7 6 5 4 3 2 1

OPM

Forever Yours is an imprint of Grand Central Publishing.

ISBN 978-1-4555-6423-1 (pbk.)

For the Chief, my own Sterling Archer.

Blowback

CHAPTER ONE

There was nothing like floating into an exclusive European cocktail party dressed in a beautiful Marchesa dress and borrowed Jimmy Choos, looking and feeling like someone in a James Bond movie.

Unfortunately, Molly would never know what that felt like. Still clutching the lost-baggage receipt the airline rep had given her, she shook her head and looked at her scuffed sneakers. Why, oh why, had she dressed like a bum to travel? She knew the answer. Archaeologists never wore anything they didn't mind getting ripped and dirty—too many excavation directors made people work as soon as they arrived—it had just been force of habit. At least her nails were clean this time.

The Athens-bound taxi bounced over a pothole, and Victoria Ruskin, a stringer for some East Coast channel who Molly had been sitting next to in the plane, bashed her head on the roof of the cab.

"Sonofa..."

"Seatbelt?" Molly said pulling at her strap and raising her eyebrows.

Rubbing her head, Victoria said, "I think you should just skip the cocktail party and come hang out at the Media Club. At least jeans are the norm there. And the dirtier they are, the more hardcore you look."

Molly didn't know what to say. She wanted to go to the Media Club with her new friend and forgo the embarrassment of turning up at a black-tie event in jeans, sneakers, and a HISTORY ROCKS T-shirt she'd picked up at a geology conference. But she couldn't. She was on a mission.

Not like a mission to seduce or a mission to stun. A real mission. A government-requested goddamn mission that she was about to completely flunk.

"I can't. I have to at least show my face," Molly said, staring out at the city lights wondering how everything could have gone so wrong so quickly.

"Seriously, you do not want to miss the war stories of the guys at the Club. And besides, there'll be plenty more cocktail parties to go to during the *endless* freaking weeks of the G20 meetings. At least two every day. You'll have plenty of time to wear your fancy dress."

Molly sighed. She was only supposed to be in Athens for a few days, but it felt futile to explain. "I know." She changed the subject. "So how long are you here covering the G20? What's your main event?" Most of the week was boring meetings of international rules regarding antiquities, energy development, and banking. Nothing, Molly imagined, that made for exciting TV. Oh God, was she trying to think like a spy now? She mentally rolled her eyes at herself.

"Oh…I'm here for the fracking discussion in the energy development sessions," Victoria said. "Three scientists are speaking for the first time about measured effects on the environment, and because we're just about to do a major vote on it in our viewer area, my channel wants me here to see if someone's actually figured out whether or not fracking is safe. Glamorous, right?"

Molly wiggled her toes in her shoes. "We sure are living the dream, aren't we?" She gave a rueful smile. Victoria seemed nice, and she was happy to have met her on the flight and to have figured out that they were both heading for the same fancy hotel. She just wished that she could get this stupid mission-slash-favor out of the way so she could go back to panicking about the speech she was scheduled to give at the antiquities meeting. And since that wasn't happening until Thursday, she also had plenty of time to hang out with Victoria at the Media Club, wherever that was. It sounded fun.

"So, the Media Club?" Victoria asked again, as the taxi ground to a halt outside the huge hotel opposite the government palace.

"I'd love to later in the week. Maybe I'll catch up with you at breakfast tomorrow and we can compare our schedules?"

Victoria looked disappointed. "Sure, maybe I'll see you later." She slipped Molly some euros for the taxi and said, "It's on me. I bet I have a bigger expense account than you."

"That wouldn't be hard, because I don't have even a small one." Molly laughed and watched as the journalist followed the porter carrying her bags into the hotel. She paid the taxi driver, hauled her paltry duffel bag on to her shoulder and walked into the ornate hotel. She *had* to learn to pack better. Jimmy Choo and Marchesa deserved carry-on baggage status, at the very least.

She checked her phone again, hoping she'd messed up on her time zone calculations. No, unfortunately not. And still no text. She bit her lip. Dr. Doubrov, the Russian antiquities minister, was only at the meeting for this one day. It had been made very clear to her that this cocktail party was going to be her only opportunity to slip him the note that she'd been given. And she was already two hours late.

She still couldn't believe she'd agreed to do this. When Brandon had first called her a week ago, she'd thought he wanted to ask her for a date. After all, he'd spent a lot of time with the team that had debriefed her for the State Department's official report on her last trip to Iraq. But no, turned out he wanted a different kind of favor. Just a small task, he'd said. One that would help her country immensely.

Of course she'd said yes. After her time with various military and ex-military people the previous year in Iraq, she'd been proud to be asked. Of course, the only answer had been yes. They met on the steps of the Lincoln Memorial, where he gave her a message to pass to Dr. Doubrov. "What on earth? Can't you just send him an email?" she'd asked.

"The Russians moved back to paper and ink about five years ago to ensure none of their secrets could get hacked," Brandon had explained. "The KGB—or the SVR as they are now—almost exclusively use typewriters now. He'd never take a thumb drive or anything that could compromise him. The only way for me to reach him is through you. You already know him, and you're already scheduled to attend the only party he's attending. No one will get suspicious about old friends chatting."

"So what's the message?"

He slipped her two plain, small envelopes, one with her first name on it, and one with her last name on it. "I'll text you with one word before you get there. Just open the corresponding envelope, read it, and recount it word for word to Doubrov when you see him. Then destroy both the envelopes afterward."

It all seemed so...*Bourne Identity*-ish.

But exciting though.

"Make sure no one overhears you talking to Doubrov. He usually has bodyguards, so get close enough for it to be a private conversation." His voice was getting tighter and more clipped the more he spoke. He seemed stressed to her. A single drop of sweat trickled diagonally across his temple. It was warm, but it wasn't that warm. His fingers danced on his leg as if he were playing an imaginary piano.

"Are you okay?" she asked in a low voice. "You look...tense?" Her mind raced, wondering what was so important that he would ask someone who could only really be described as a remote acquaintance to help him out.

He frowned at her. "What are you talking about? I'm just asking you to do a simple thing for me. For your country."

"But last year, when I met you, you were—and please know I mean no disrespect—a fairly junior State Department officer, bringing tea and taking notes. This feels…strange."

"I know it does, and I'm sorry. I've just become party to some information that needs to be passed on to someone in the Russian government without a big deal being made of it. I'm still trying to pin down the details, which is why you have two envelopes. I'm waiting for one last confirmation, but that won't come until you are in the air. But don't worry. You're perfect for the job." A smile reached his eyes briefly. "I know you, and you know Doubrov, and no one's going to think twice about you talking to him. It actually works all around."

It sounded absolutely reasonable when he put it like that. She did know Dr. Doubrov, and had found him to be a passionate scholar of archaeology and antiquities. He only ever had one speaking mode, and that was a full-on lecture. He'd lecture anyone about anything, but always with a twinkle in his eye, knowing full well that his imposing six-foot-plus stature intimidated people. As did his nationality and his alleged past in the KGB. But he'd always seemed to have a good sense of humor, and Molly liked what she knew about him. She also knew that he'd be happy to see her again, because he'd told her boss as much on the phone a month ago. Harry had told her to be sure to look to him for support during her speech if necessary.

Some of her early speeches had gone down less well, with academic heckling and private contractors trying to diminish her experiences. But as they went along, she'd become more adept at handling them. But at an event this important, she was happy to have someone very well thought of to have her back if necessary.

She'd tucked the two envelopes into her purse, tamping down the exhilaration rushing through her. Did this make her a spy? She'd really thought it might. She'd raised her eyes expectantly, silently asking if there was anything else.

"Good girl," he'd said, which had made her bristle. *Girl?* She'd let it slide with the sudden realization that for a short couple of days, she'd be an agent. A real government agent. Excitement had coursed through her that her country—the US of freaking A—would trust her with such an important task. Her, a mere archaeologist.

"Remember. You have a four-hour window at that cocktail party. Don't miss him. The consequences will be dire if you don't get the message to him. Like two-superpowers-going-to-war dire." And then he'd jumped up and walked away, without so much as a thank you or a good luck.

But Molly hadn't cared. She'd sat there for a good ten minutes gazing out at the Washington Monument and reveling in the fact that she had been called to serve her country.

It was going to be epic. A story to tell her grandkids.

But for now, she was still late. She checked in and took the elevator to her room, pausing only to throw her small bag over the threshold into the room before running back toward the elevator. She checked her phone again. Still no text. Shit. She had both envelopes in her jeans pocket. She just needed to know which one to open. She followed the signs for the party and headed to the back of the hotel.

There was a security team, patting down guests and funneling them through metal detectors. When they came to Molly, the man in black's eyebrows raised. "Lost luggage," she said, giving him a rueful smile and flashing her "Guest Speaker" pass.

"I'm sure no one will notice," he said with an utterly charming Greek accent. She looked at his nametag.

"That's so sweet of you, Platon Asker. Thank you." She felt better already. Especially since Platon was tall and good looking. *Very* good looking. That didn't hurt.

The party was everything she'd hoped for—glamorous women floating in long dresses and smart men in tuxes. Champagne flutes and night sky. Tall arrangements of flowers arching toward the stars. Breathtaking. It seemed as if the restaurant had retracted its whole roof and allowed the entire area out to the balcony to be open air. She wished so hard that she were wearing her dress and sexy high heels.

Her butt vibrated. *At last.* She dug out her phone.

Molly.

She grabbed a glass of champagne from a tray and circled the guests to locate Dr. Doubrov.

David Church eyed the people talking to his principal. Close protection was a bitch, but the company he worked for had saved him from self-destruction, so he basically owed them his soul. And this week, his soul was guarding a very important scientist. He had no idea who would want to hurt a scientist, but his boss had assigned him to Athens, and here he was.

Although his attention was on Professor Rankin, he was also scanning the room for someone special, the other reason he hadn't complained at taking this job: Molly Solent was on the week's schedule, and he wanted to see her.

Badly. Like blue-balls badly.

He'd kept track of her for nearly a year, since they'd met, briefly, in Iraq. At the time he'd been in no shape to choose a tie color, let alone date someone as...*unique* as Molly.

From the second he'd laid eyes on her, he knew she was trouble. Trouble for him, anyway. His eyes rested for a second on the far wall, which was adorned with a mosaic picture of an ancient Greek warrior. In some way he was like that mosaic. A fine illustration of a fighter, but when you got up close, you could see the cracks. Millions of cracks. Good for no one, especially someone like Molly. Hell, he was barely in good enough shape to have this job. But his CEO had seen something in him—or so he'd said—something that David couldn't see himself, and had sent him on a series of low-risk jobs. It had been almost enough to take his mind off Molly.

She had haunted his days and nights with her eyes that were full of promise, full of a future than he couldn't see. She'd seen him at his worst, and it didn't seem to faze her at all. Her eyes. He closed his own as he thought about her again. Innocent and totally open. She'd wanted him and hadn't been afraid at all of making it clear.

Her image had kept him going through the long, dark nights of recovery. The single chink of light in his life. He was scared to lose that. Scared to see her.

The one thing that he was proud of, pretty much the only thing, was walking away from her before he sucked her into his downward spiral.

He had to keep his mind on that one point if he saw her here. He wasn't fixed yet. Wasn't entirely right. He still looked longingly at liquor, remembering the peace that came at the bottom of the bottle. He still dreamed that he'd fallen off the wagon. When he woke up, all he could remember is how good it felt. And the hallucinations. Nope. He definitely wasn't ready for Molly. And she definitely didn't deserve the shit-storm that seemed to always revolve around him.

The professor moved to speak to someone else, and David snapped back into alertness. He scanned the immediate crowd around him. No threats. But he couldn't relax. She could be here. Molly could be right here, in the same room as him. He ran a finger under his collar as his temperature rose.

He'd known she would be here, but he still hadn't decided whether to speak to her. And he'd had two months to think about it. Seeing her would be enough, he was sure. Just to rest his eyes on her again, even without her knowing, would fulfill nearly a year of longing.

He hoped.

Because he was knockdown sure as shit convinced that if he spoke to her, looked into her eyes, felt her soft skin again, he would be a goner. And he knew very well that he would stop at nothing to get her into his arms, his bed, and his life. So it was by far the best bet that he not draw attention to the fact that he was there. He could see her, yet she wouldn't see him. Distance was his friend. Distance and the lotion back in his room.

He took a sip of the ice water he was cradling. The professor was talking to two old guys who were almost busting out of their dress shirts. They seemed to be exchanging stories and laughing, one of them puffing on a cigar. He allowed himself a glance around the room.

And then everything went still.

Molly.

He closed his eyes momentarily. It was a hallucination. He was wise to them by now. She was in jeans and a T-shirt, which were the only clothes he'd ever seen her in. If she were real, she'd be in a beautiful cocktail dress. He shook his head and focused on his principal. He breathed in and out, in and out. Concentrated on the professor. Mentally he recited the things he knew about him.

His wife's name is Cathy.

His office is on University Boulevard.

He went to Cornell.

He looked briefly for signs of Molly again but couldn't see her. The focus technique had worked its magic.

He caught sight of Malone Garrett, his partner in crime on this job. A British son of a bitch who never took anything seriously and was perpetually ready with some smartass comment. He had his eyes on his own principal, an oil guy who'd been a target of some environmental activists, but he was drinking what looked like bourbon on the rocks. He'd heard rumors that Mal was ex-SAS—Special Air Service, the regiment that Delta Force was modeled on—which made him pretty damn hardcore, but David also knew he had his own rumors doing the circuit in his new company, and not all of those were true.

Mal grinned and raised his drink when he caught David's gaze on him. David raised his water glass back and rolled his eyes. Even drinking, Mal was on top of his game. Lucky bastard, being able to function like that. And he looked annoyingly crisp in his tux. David felt hot and uncomfortable in his.

He couldn't wait to take it off. The Brit must have some James Bond gene. God, that pissed him off.

His principal moved out onto the terraces, where gas lamps offered a yellow glow to complement the brutal heat of the evening. He pushed nearer to the professor so that he could clearly see the hands and posture of the people around him.

He noticed a few bodyguards who were obviously packing weapons. With their bulging shoulders and virtually shaved heads, he tagged them as Russian. In the private security world, it paid to be able to identify other bodyguards. It was always good to know who you could go to for assistance if necessary. And it was good to know who you definitely couldn't go to. The Russians were in the latter category.

Their principal seemed to be an older man who was ignoring them. David didn't blame him. His bodyguards seemed to be scaring off anyone who might have wanted to talk to him. He just puffed his pipe and looked around hopefully. David saw his eyes light up. Good for him. He'd found someone to talk to.

David's attention snapped back to the professor, and then back to the Russian. He blinked. Molly-in-jeans was kissing him. He blinked again. It really was her. He was sure of it. A warmth washed over him, tempered only by a tightening in his stomach. Even in jeans, and a T-shirt that had seen better days, she put the glamorously dressed women there in the shade.

But what was she doing? Both Molly and the Russian were looking down at their clasped hands. One of them was obviously being overfriendly. He smiled. David bet that the Russian was so happy to have someone talk to him, he didn't want to let her go. But then he seemed to pull his hand free and something dropped to the ground. Molly swooped down to pick it up, and as she did, David saw a red flower bloom on the Russian's chest.

Before even mentally registering what was happening, David stepped toward the professor and grabbed his arm. He saw Mal moving toward his principal too. Neither of the Russian bodyguards had even flinched.

But David hesitated, eyes on Molly as she started to pull herself upright.

Someone screamed, and the guests looked at the source. He had about two seconds until mass panic. But he couldn't leave Molly. He spoke into his cuff mike to Mal. "Take the professor." He knew that would piss Mal off, but he'd still do it. As David stepped to Molly, who was looking blankly at the Russian as he slumped to his knees, he saw Mal yanking the professor behind the bar in his peripheral vision. Another shot splattered one of the huge vases close to Molly. The cracking glass made more noise than the gunshot. He flung himself at her and brought her down to the ground, covering her with his body. The noise of the shattering glass brought the crowd from a polite murmur to shrieks of panic in about a second and a half.

Instead of lying prone, she tried to wriggle away from him, closer to the dead Russian. "Molly. *Molly.* Stop," he said. But she acted like she didn't hear him. She reached for something and stuffed it in her pocket.

"Come on. We have to get out of here." He jumped up and dragged her behind the bar. There were no more shots, but people were running in panic. He looked to the entrance of the party and saw Mal with his oil exec and Professor Rankin speeding back through the metal detector. As Mal walked them through the doorway, he grabbed a bottle of Kristal champagne from a table. Typical. A couple of seconds later the entrance was a bottleneck of people pushing and shoving to get away from whatever was going down.

He grabbed Molly's hand and pushed her toward the emergency exit door into the kitchen. It was deserted except for one cleaner, who was looking bemused. "Go!" David said, pointing at the exit door. The man dropped his mop and disappeared.

"David? David?" Molly said breathlessly, as they burst through the service entrance.

"Hang on," he replied, not wanting to have that particular conversation here. He peered around the corner of the corridor and saw police running past a door at the end. He waited until the steady stream of white riot-helmets passed, and then he ran to the door and checked. No one.

"Molly!" he called.

No answer. He looked over his shoulder. Shit. Racing back to around the corner, he promised God everything if she was still alive. She was, but she was crouched down, arms wrapped around her knees. "Molly? We have to go."

She didn't look at him, and didn't reply. Fuck this. They didn't have time for hysteria. He picked her up in his arms, and only then noticed a patch of blood on the wall where she'd been sitting. Her face buried in his neck, he looked at his hand. It was red too.

Three minutes later she was in his room. He laid her on his

bed and rolled her over on to her side. Her T-shirt was soaked in blood.

A coldness rushed through him. Had she been shot too? He was just about to lift her shirt, when a voice spoke in his ear, scaring the shit out of him.

"So who's Molly?" Mal asked through his earpiece.

"A woman," he said tightly.

"No shit, Sherlock. Anyway, I've got your principal. Nuts of steel that guy's got. My oil exec, on the other hand, has fled for his private jet."

"Thanks for that. How's the Kristal?"

"Delicious. So who was the dead dude?"

David's jaw tightened. "I don't know. I'm waiting to ask Molly, but she's bleeding and maybe catatonic or something.

"Am not," she mumbled.

"Bleeding from what?" Mal asked.

"Her skin." His voice rose in exasperation. "Shut up. I'm looking."

"No need to get your knickers in a twist. Wait. Is she conscious? Are you feeling up an unconscious woman?" He could hear that bastard's grin.

"Shut the fuck up," David said.

"Don't speak to me like that," Molly said, a little more strength behind her words this time.

"A little testy, mate, aren't you?"

Shit. David pulled his earpiece out and threw it in the trash.

"Molly, you're bleeding from something, I'm just trying to see where from. Do you remember being shot?" he asked, feeling a bit stupid for asking.

"I think I'd remember that," she replied, rolling back to look at him. "David. It really is…Ow!" She sat upright nearly head butting him in the process. "Something's stabby there." She gestured around her back.

"Lie back down and let me see. And yes, it's really me."

She mumbled something into his pillow as he pulled up her shirt all the way to her shoulder. He grit his teeth. Molly had a line of glass shrapnel down her back. Nothing that he couldn't deal with himself, maybe five shards, but still, he couldn't believe she wasn't screaming the hotel down. He needed to take advantage of the adrenaline while it was numbing her to the injury. "What did you say?"

She pulled herself to her elbows and turned to look at him over her shoulder. "I said, 'You said you'd come for me.'"

"What?" He grabbed his first aid kit out of his bag and lightly pushed her back down. Grabbing a pair of forceps and gauze, he set about removing the glass.

She just groaned. Good job too. He'd heard what she said, and it bit him to his core. When he'd last seen her at the airport in Iraq, he'd told her that he'd come for her. They'd had such an intense connection, albeit totally platonic, that he'd been sure that he would be looking her up as soon as he got stateside. But his sober, in-recovery head had prevailed. He'd struggled when he got back stateside. He was hauled over the coals by the Feds and then became instrumental in bringing down the black-ops company he'd worked for.

He'd left the dark side, and maybe he should have found Molly, but something had held him back. He'd realized that she was better off without his fucked-up self hanging around.

Now she was here, he couldn't imagine how he'd convinced himself of that. How he'd stayed away for so long. She was still…perfect. Well, bleeding, obviously, but perfect nonetheless. He had to keep his head in the game. The original plan: stay away from her. He didn't deserve her, and she definitely didn't deserve a broken, ex-military guy with no foreseeable future. Especially since he'd just effectively deserted his post.

No. He had to keep her at arm's length. The level of his attraction to her in Iraq had shocked him, rattled him to his core. But he'd been involved with such shady activities, he'd barely spoken to her. Barely spoken to anyone. Now, for sure, he was better. But the darkness still lurked. The memories of the deaths of friends, the nightmares, and cold sweats that came from nowhere. She'd never understand what he'd done. No one could.

He barely could.

The last of the glass was out, and he sprayed an antibiotic ointment over the little cuts, and fixed a makeshift bandage with gauze and tape. "There. Good as new. Kind of."

She sat up. Shit, her face was so white.

"Are you going to pass out?" he asked, concerned.

He shoved her head between her legs and held her down with his hand between her shoulder blades. She relaxed beneath his hand, and he found himself stroking her shoulders.

Her head popped up. Followed by the rest of her. She was at the door before he had time to react. "Dr. Doubrov. I have to find him. It's important."

CHAPTER TWO

Molly felt for her pocket. The envelopes were still there, thank God. She opened the door, but David slammed it shut.

"I'll just be a few minutes. I just have to see Dr. Doubrov. It's important."

"Is that the guy you were holding hands with? He was shot, sweetheart." He frowned at her.

Molly took a moment. Yes. He'd fallen down. He'd been shot? "Who shot him?"

David was silent for a moment, and her gaze rested on his face.

David. Here.

Hell, he looked good. All these months waiting for him, and he was just here.

When she had first really laid eyes on him, she was peeking at him through a window as he took an impossible shot into a trailer and saved them. He'd been drunk, and impossible. And she'd wanted him so much. Wanted to save him, to make him feel better. To stomp on whatever demons were keeping him from participating in reality. To run her fingers through his short dark hair. His eyes had been so sad, and he'd seemed resigned. Like he'd already given up on life. In that second he'd broken her heart as he'd saved her life.

It hadn't hurt that he was tall, and built in the way only a career combat military guy could be. Broad shouldered, with hard arms that she just wanted to be wrapped in. When his dark eyes had rested on hers, the hard lines on his face faded, and although his lips remained pressed into a hard line, his eyes had smiled at her. She thought. Maybe she hoped.

Right now, all she could think of was that she wanted to touch his face. To kiss him. To understand what had happened to him, and what had changed. And he had changed. He seemed more in control, sober, obviously. He spoke with a lower voice. Seemed less...something. She couldn't put her finger on the change. Her hand reached out to him, but she snatched it back before she could touch him.

She was on a mission. She was supposed to destroy the envelope she didn't use, but in the end she hadn't had time to give him either of the messages, so she figured she should keep them, but everything was getting confused in her mind. Should she destroy them both? Is there someone else she should give the message to? She had to keep working through the problem. If she stopped, she feared she'd break down and might never be able to pull herself together. She didn't want him to witness that. She clenched her fists.

"Who was he?" David asked.

"He's the Russian minister of antiquities. Alexandre Doubrov. Why would someone…?"

"I have no idea," he said, leading her back to the bed. "But you're not going anywhere. There was no way he'd have been able to survive that shot. I'm sorry."

She nodded but said nothing. He'd died right in front of her. Poor Alexandre. She had to get hold of Brandon to tell him she'd failed. But she wanted the whole picture before she called him. She yawned. Suddenly sleepy.

"So what have you been doing this past year?" David said, his voice seeming miles away.

Her mind immediately went to the airport at Iraq, as it had a million times before. He'd grabbed her and roughly pulled her into his arms, telling her that he would find her and come for her. Then he'd kissed her forehead hard and departed with his old team of explosive experts on a mission, leaving her to return to the states. Damn him.

"What have *you* been doing since we met last?" she asked sluggishly.

He sat across the room from her in an armchair. "Giving evidence, getting my shit back together, you know, the usual." He dragged the chair closer to the bed, still keeping his distance.

Her mind wasn't really in the room. She was picturing Alexandre's face as he'd caught sight of her. How his face had lit up, happy to see her there. How he'd kissed her cheeks and then how he'd jumped, a little startled, when he'd felt the contraband being exchanged. And then…he'd been shot. In front of her. Was it *because* of her? Suddenly she realized she was cold. A few seconds later she was shivering uncontrollably. Her brain ceased to work...at least in any meaningful way. All she wanted to do was get warm.

"Get in." David gestured to the bed. She didn't need to be asked twice. The huge fluffy duvet was calling to her, but she couldn't seem to move. "You're probably going into shock, Molly." She felt his hands pushing her down.

"How back together is your shit, then?" she mumbled, fast losing the threads of consciousness.

"Not very," his voice came from far away.

When she awoke, David was asleep in the armchair. She bit back a groan as she sat up. Her cuts stung like a motherfucker. She'd been cut by the vase, which had been shattered by the guy who'd shot her friend. She took a steadying breath. Okay. She could do this. Her country had asked her to step up, and she'd tried her best. But she wasn't done. She hadn't failed...yet.

She grabbed her phone and looked for Brandon's number so she could text him. A quick glance told her that David was still asleep.

Mission not accomplished. Mission Impossible.

Crap, she couldn't say that. She didn't really know what to say. Maybe that was too much. Maybe someone was monitoring her phone. Was she paranoid? Getting too far into this? She deleted it and tried again.

Cocktail party was a bust.

There. No one could read more into that, surely. Besides which, a shooting at a G20 cocktail party was bound to be covered by all the news channels. She hit SEND and watched for a reply. Nothing. She pulled the envelopes from her pocket and felt them under the duvet. Was the message to blame for the shooting? Maybe it was a warning that he was going to be killed and she'd arrived too damn late to save him? *Stupid effing airline.*

"How do you feel?" David said, his voice making her jump.

"I don't know how to answer that," she said, gingerly leaning back onto the pillows. "My back hurts, my friend…well my acquaintance, is dead, and I guess it could easily have been me, right? I mean if you hadn't jumped on me?"

He stretched his arms above his head and she heard a series of clicks as his joints cracked. She winced at his grimace. And something in her softened. She wanted to touch him, to ease his pain, his past. A wave of warmth flooded through her as she watched him awaken properly. No, she couldn't think that way again. He'd already broken one promise to her, she wasn't going to get sucked into him again. But…she was alone in a hotel room with him.

"Don't look at me like that, sweetheart," he said.

"Like what?"

He gave her a "you know what I mean" look.

Before she could say anything, a weird vibration came from the other side of the room. A tinny voice. "Um, I think your trash can is talking. That's…not right…right?" She held her head. This was all so surreal that there had to be a good chance that she was dreaming, or maybe locked in an asylum somewhere having a very specific delusion. David being in Greece, Alexandre being shot, the stupid message she hadn't passed. No one could blame her for taking a second to see if things were actually real. She rubbed her eyes and shook her head.

David pinched her as he went by. "Yup. It's all real."

She opened her eyes, solely with the purpose of eye-rolling him, and saw him fish something out of the wastebasket and stick it in his ear. It took her a second. *Oh, right.* Must be an earpiece. Which kind of explained the fractured conversation she vaguely remembered from last night. Last night…

David shoved the earpiece in his ear. "What's up?"

"Do you want to go on a field trip?" Mal asked.

How was he not hung over and still sleeping? That guy had the constitution of an ox. An ox on PCP.

"I'm kind of tied up right now," David said, stretching again and shutting the bathroom door behind him.

"Nice work, mate. Wait. Literally tied up? You need help, or privacy?"

There was just no talking to him.

"What field trip?"

"To the sniper's lair."

A jolt flashed through him. "Yeah. That's the sort of field trip I'm interested in."

"You know the proper answer to that question should have been 'No, we'll let the authorities handle it'?"

"I'm not proper," David said. Mal was right, but this felt personal now. He wanted to get answers for Molly. If nothing else, he could give her that.

"I thought you might not be. Meet me in the lobby in ten."

"Roger that." David took the earpiece out and eyed the shower. He was still in his suit pants and shirt from the night before. He needed to change. Nothing said "guy we need to question" like a disheveled guy in a tux following a night of death and destruction.

Eight minutes later, he emerged from the bathroom in jeans and a T-shirt, thinking about what he needed to take with him on the field trip. And then he remembered. Molly. Sweet, crazy, and injured Molly. What had she been trying to pass the Russian before he'd been shot? He had a concern that she was into something bad. He'd definitely witnessed the attempted pass. He didn't imagine that. He didn't think. But then he hadn't believed Molly was actually there, even when he'd seen her. Maybe he was still teetering on the edge of insanity.

"Where are you going?" Molly asked from the bed.

She was lying back down again, on her side, looking sleepy. He grabbed a bottle of military-grade ibuprofen from his bag and shook out a horse pill. "Here. Take this before you sleep. I'll be back in a couple of hours, okay?"

She nodded, and as she took the pill and glass of water, he fought every instinct to crawl in beside her, and wrap his arms around her as she slept. He'd killed someone to save her life in Iraq, and that had to mean something. She was his to protect now. What the hell was she into? Or was she just in the wrong place at the wrong time? He wanted to know what was in her head. Why her eyes had lost that glow of openness he'd remembered. He wanted her so badly. Had been wanting her for months. He shook his head and reined in his impulse.

"Don't go anywhere. I'll wake you when I get back." He hesitated and leaned down, swiftly pressing his lips to her forehead. He let himself out of the room and braced the door as it closed so the bang wouldn't startle her, hanging the DO NOT DISTURB sign on the handle.

In the lobby, Mal was drinking coffee from an impossibly small cup and reading a newspaper. He didn't acknowledge David's presence.

David pulled out his phone and pretended to scroll through emails as he surveyed the foyer. There were two policemen behind the reception desk looking at a computer and one talking to the concierge. David stowed his phone and strode out of the hotel, snagging some tourist brochures from the concierge desk, figuring brazenness would save the day. It worked. Both the hotel employee and the policeman smiled at him as he left. You could get away with anything ninety-nine percent of the time if you smiled and appeared relaxed.

He hooked a left outside the hotel and loitered by a newspaper bodega. To his alarm, the English newspapers all led with the assassination of a Russian official at the G20 meeting. The Greeks were outraged that this had happened on their turf, and all the other coverage was speculating on why a minister of antiquities was the target.

"Not exactly low profile," Malone said from behind him.

David just nodded and walked toward the next block. As soon as they were out of earshot of the bodega guy, Mal pointed to the left, and they took the road that led to the back of the hotel.

"So, who's the bird?" he asked.

Of course that would be the first thing he mentioned. "Just someone I met last year."

"Pre, or post fucked-up breakdown?" he asked boldly.

David shot him a look, trying to figure out the line of questioning. He wasn't one hundred percent sure about Molly and what she was doing last night, but that was his problem and he wasn't going to lay her open for Mal to investigate. He paused, not willing to suggest that she had anything to do with the situation, nor wanting to lie.

"Look. It's no secret you were totally fucked up last year. I don't mean anything by that…we've all been fucked over at some time in the last ten years. That's war for you. All hot girls, dancing, and booze. Bound to get to a bloke eventually. But the thing is: you froze. You had one fraction of a second of indecision, and then you left your principal. Because of her. So I'm going to ask you again. Is she part of the bad stuff that you went through last year, or part of the recovery?"

David got it. Mal was asking if he needed to get involved to stop David crashing again. He'd have asked the same thing. "She's neither actually. She was an innocent bystander in Iraq last year. We had some kind of connect—"

"All right, mate. I don't need you to get mushy on me. I just need to know that she's not going to be a problem for us."

He decided to come clean-ish. "She's an archaeologist. A speaker at the conference. I knew she was coming, but I didn't plan on making contact with her again. She knew the vic and went to greet him, which is when he was shot. That's pretty much all I know right now. I'm mostly sure she's not going to be a problem."

"Mostly. That's terrific. Mostly. There's a lot of potential crap in that word, you know." Mal increased his stride as they crossed another road.

"I swear, man. Not a problem." He sounded more confident of his answer this time, but maybe he still hadn't been convincing enough.

Mal gave him a fast look of barely hidden disbelief. David couldn't blame him. Unfortunately he couldn't be sure of anything, especially that she was any less of a problem than the police presence at the building. He didn't want anyone diving into his background, and he suspected his boss didn't either. He guessed they'd have to get into the sniper's lair some other way.

But Mal's brain was clearly back on the mission at hand. He didn't hesitate. He directed David through a short alleyway that took them into a courtyard of the adjacent building.

Ignoring three doorways, Mal opened the fourth and took the steps behind it two at a time. *Holy shit.* Mal had been up long enough to scope out the area. David felt ashamed that he'd stayed in the room so long. But Molly. He'd stayed up way too long watching her sleep.

"Okay," Mal kept his voice low. "This is the floor that the police have cordoned off, next door. It's directly opposite the hotel restaurant." He paused.

David looked out of the open stairwell and thought about the night before. He used his hands to visualize the trajectory of the sniper's bullet. "No. I'd say the bullet hit the Russian at a forty-five degree angle, blowing out his lower back. Which means..." he looked up and across at the restaurant. "I'd say the nest is maybe two floors higher."

Malone looked relieved. "Thank God. They said you were

solid, but you know, after last night…" He held his hand flat and shifted it to and fro.

"You dick. I'd heard it was you I had to keep my eye on."

Mal smiled. "You should. If you want to learn something. Come on. Stop wasting time." He strode up the remaining steps to the roof. Once there, it was easy to step across a small wall on to the roof of the next-door building.

David spotted a door and nodded toward it. He reached it first, and pulled on the handle. Locked. "Of course." He breathed, taking out his knife.

Mal watched the surrounding roofs as David levered the door open by forcing the blade through the doorjamb. It was relatively easy. Nothing up here seemed to have been well maintained, and the wood splintered as if it hadn't seen a lick of moisture in decades.

Three floors down they found the likely lair. Both men stood in the doorway listening to the sounds of the police a couple of floors down. Mal raised his eyebrows at the laughing below, and David just shook his head.

The room was empty. The floor was covered in linoleum that had seen better days. A couple of boxes lay near the window, and several others by the wall. Mal stared toward them. They appeared empty, but who knew?

The sun peeking through the window glinted on something. "Stop!" David hissed. Mal stopped dead in his tracks and looked to find the reason for David's order.

"Tripwire about ten inches from your left foot." David approached and followed the wire to the wall. "Huh."

"Huh what?" Mal said through gritted teeth.

"Wait." The tripwire disappeared on both sides of the room under what appeared to be empty boxes. Then extended in a V shape to the boxes in front of the window. "Back up toward the door. Try not to deviate from where you were before." He heard Mal sigh, but was grateful that he complied. As he lifted the cardboard boxes he saw devices with enough explosives to wipe out the room, but not much else. Probably not the people inside the room either. Weird. Just enough to destroy the evidence, he guessed, but not enough to kill anyone. Someone with some explosive skills had great restraint. Usually people who made their living designing bombs did so for maximum mayhem. This bomb maker was clearly very specific about the level of destruction he desired. Or he was under specific orders.

David couldn't detach the wire without triggering the explosive charge, so he shrugged and cut the plastic wire in two places to relieve the tension on the trigger. He walked around slowly, ensuring there were no secondary devices. "All clear."

"Tell me before you cut a wire next time, mate. You nearly gave me a heart attack. I thought in these situations we're supposed to have a hilarious conversation about which to cut: the blue or the red wire. Don't just snip something without discussing it first, okay?"

It was hard to tell how serious Mal was about anything. "It wasn't wire." He picked it up and sniffed it. "It's minty dental floss." He frowned and sniffed again. "Wow. That's…really improvised. The whole thing feels unplanned. Like someone wasn't expecting to have to rig something but managed to anyway. That's…hardcore." He met Mal's eyes.

Mal nodded. "And hardcore means fanatic or professional. Neither one fills the heart with moonlight and roses."

Suddenly, voices came from a few floors down. Raised and excitable. Mal and David rushed to the window and looked down. As soon as they did, a muffled boom launched a wave of dust and glass through a lower window. Then before they could do much more than wince, the window below theirs blew out too. They looked at each other for a second. Mal braced himself as if he was expecting their room to blow too.

David raised an eyebrow. "You saw me defuse it right?"

"Sure I did. But I don't know how good you are at that shit. You could be crap."

"Well let's see how good you are. Get us out of here with as much evidence as you can." He looked back toward the door. "I'd say we have less than a minute to clear the building.

Mal didn't hesitate. He stacked one empty box inside another, set it in the middle of the floor and started throwing things in it. David grabbed as much dental floss as he could, the device, and the explosives. He lobbed all but the explosives into the box. Those he tucked in his jacket pocket.

A second later the room upstairs blew too. "Okay, we've got to go *now*."

David lofted the box full of evidence and broke for the stairwell. Below, he could see men in antiexplosive suits slowly advancing on them. They must be the police's bomb squad. A good half of him wanted to stop and shoot the shit with them. He missed the craziness of the Air Force Explosive Ordnance Disposal guys. Instead he took the stairs two by two. Mal was now ahead of him, as he hadn't stopped to look at the bomb squad.

David stopped on the next floor up, where bomb debris had blown into the stairwell. He picked up some larger pieces and stuffed them in a pocket and kept running. Once on the roof, they retraced their steps back to the building adjacent.

As soon as they were inside the building, they stopped to take a breath. "Jesus. Every floor?" Mal said.

"Someone really wanted to cover their tracks. But I have to say, to me that sounds like more than one person. Setting four bombs on tripwire takes time. It's not something you can do fast. I mean unless they set them all earlier...but then they ran the risk of them blowing before the hit." David frowned as they walked much slower down the second flight of stairs.

"Bombs are pretty commonplace here," Mal said slowly.

"Huh?"

"I mean people aren't as freaked out by them here. Athens has a healthy population of antiestablishment anarchists of all stripes. Hell, just this year they've firebombed a few American businesses. Never heard of them using a sniper though."

"So it could be someone sent to assassinate the Russian minister and using bombs to make the authorities think they're local anarchists?" David said. "Sounds clumsy to me. No way would they think those bombs were from anarchists. Well, depending, I guess, on what's left of them now. From what I could see, a hefty amount of evidence shot out of the window."

"The bad news is that they will go to see why our floor didn't blow out too. Footprints, fibers, fingerprints. Shit. I touched the window frame when the second floor blew," Mal said.

David knew that everything he'd touched was in the box he held. "Dammit. Well you probably have about three days before they process the prints."

"I'm not in the system. But it still doesn't fill me with the joys of spring to know that anyone has my fingerprints." He fell silent, and David allowed him a few minutes to digest. If Mal *was* SAS, his prints would definitely be classified. But with the world's eyes on Athens and the G20 meeting, there may be pressured cooperation between the countries. Which meant Mal's days in Athens was numbered. He was sure Mal was thinking about that.

"The worst thing isn't that my identity will be blown, it's that the authorities will think the British had something to do with the assassination of a Russian minister. And frankly, boy-o, you should be worried about that too. Send your girl away. Whoever she is, she'll be in their crosshairs, being the person with him when he got killed. Your country doesn't want that heat either. No offense, mate, but country first. Give her a kiss and send her to the airport. Fast."

So Mal, for all his attitude, was as patriotic to his country as David was to his. He was right on all counts, as well. David knew what he had to do. Should do.

Do I have the strength to send her away again? Yes, yes he did. He had to.

When they got to Mal's room, David laid some clean white towels on the bed and started placing the recovered items on it. As he went, he placed the bomb components together as they'd been connected in situ. The more he rebuilt, the more he concocted a vision of how this went down. Someone had left at least the explosive charge, and maybe all the equipment, for the shooter. The shooter could have set the explosives, made his shot, and then left, knowing that as soon as someone located the origin point of the shot, the evidence would be blown up. Meaning the shooter could make a fast getaway, not having to worry about clean up. Or, someone assembled the explosives after. But that would have been too risky. Actually the only scenario that made sense was that the explosives were rigged before the sniper took position. *Oh. Ohhhh.*

"Okay," David said. "Imagine you've been given the assassination job. Your front man has set up a bunch of explosives to cover any evidence you were there after you've done the job."

Mal sat in the armchair and nodded, leaning forward, elbows on knees. It was the most serious David had ever seen him.

"You're directed to the second floor to take the shot. What happens?"

Mal didn't hesitate. "I make a mental note to kill the guy who told me I could get a bead on the target from the second floor. There isn't a good enough line of vision to get a shot."

David nodded. "So the explosives are rigged on the first, second and third floors. But you need the fourth floor to make your shot."

Mal nodded. "I take the explosives from one of the other floors, and put them on the fourth floor."

"But?"

Mal was already nodding. "But to move the explosives, I

have to cut the wire. So I take the bombs onto the fourth floor, and then I have to use something else as the tripwire. Something handy...something like dental floss."

David looked back at the towel and picked up the sheath to a pen. It was a metal tube with "BP" engraved on it. Someone's initials, not a logo. "This came from the floor above. It's charred, so it was definitely near the bomb. Maybe even the contact blocker."

"Keep it in case," Mal said. "I don't much like anything going on here. Can you get rid of the explosives?"

"Sure." That wasn't even slightly difficult. He could throw it in any trash can in the city and it would be totally inert. Although he was more inclined to take them to the US embassy. "I'm going to check in on Molly."

"Great. Ask her why someone would want to shoot her friend, will ya? Could save time." Mal wrapped up the towel with all the evidence, and dumped it on the floor. He lay on the bed, and put both hands behind his head and closed his eyes.

David didn't dignify it with a reply.

CHAPTER THREE

When Molly woke, the first thing she checked was her pocket. Then her phone. The notes were still there, and the phone had no text or voice mail. Brandon Peterson had disappeared. Or disavowed her. A prickling of anxiety settled in her stomach, and she blew out air through puffed cheeks, trying to dispel the feeling.

David. She was in David's room. At last. A year she'd been looking over her shoulder, waiting for him to show up. And now she was here with him. In Athens.

She knew he was worried about her, but she hadn't done anything wrong. Maybe she'd been about to do something in service of her country, but she hadn't. And it still wasn't wrong. Her thoughts flittered to Doubrov, wondering if she had done something that led to his death.

Her head felt clear again, even though her back throbbed. She fingered the messages in her pocket. Should she read the other one too? She'd been told not to. She just wished Brandon would return her call so he could tell her what to do.

She stretched and winced again at the pull of the wounds in her back. She needed a shower and some clean clothes. Maybe her luggage had arrived. Suddenly the idea of clean underwear and clothes that didn't have slivers of glass in it was overwhelmingly attractive. She left David a note and went down to her room.

Bliss. Her suitcase had arrived. She sighed with relief and pulled out a silk blouse and a skirt, hung them on a hanger, and took them into the bathroom with her to steam out the creases. The shower was heavenly, but being alone and naked made her long for David with a heaviness that threaded through her stomach. Nervousness perhaps. She'd spent a year thinking about him, dreaming about him, wondering what she would do if he had actually called. The thought of him actually being here, causing this physical reaction in her, confused her.

She wasn't sure when she had put it all together in her head, but her boss had married Matt, the other man who'd helped them in Iraq, so it was as if her soul had accepted that David would be hers. Like a perfect and symmetrical outcome. Henrietta had Matt, and she would have David. He must have felt the same, she'd been sure. Every time they'd seen each other, his eyes would never leave hers. They burned into her, making her think that they were connected at some profound level. She was sure he saw her, really saw her. He didn't say much when he was sober, and only laughed that one time she'd seen him drunk, but they'd seemed to say so much without words that she was sure—no she *knew*—he would come for her when she returned to the US.

And when the months passed, and her feeling about the man who had rescued her, totally on top of his game even though he'd been drunk at the time, had never diminished. She waited, sure every time she got home that he'd be on her doorstep.

He was hers. Her heart had never accepted even a sliver of doubt, though he hadn't even kissed her. Two kisses on the freaking forehead were all he'd given her. Maybe if she wore heels she'd be at the right height to get a kiss where she wanted one. But he'd done nothing except hold her close at the airport a year ago. Why had she been celibate just waiting on the off chance that he'd make good on his promise? And why was washing herself in the shower making her want him with every part of her? Every drop of water felt like a touch. His touch. But now he was really here, yet different. More careful, more considered. Still intense, still dangerous. Still wildly attractive.

She shook it off by peeling the wet bandages from her back. And shampooing her hair. Hard. As she was getting out of the shower, there was a knock at the door. Her stomach fluttered. David? Who else could it be?

Excited, she wrapped a large towel around herself and ran to open the door. She checked the peephole with her hand already on the handle. Two unsmiling men stood there. Not David. She took a step back and tightened the towel around her.

The two men discussed something outside, and she leaned in so she could hear. "Open the damned door," one man with an accent said.

"No, I can't..." The second man was interrupted with an audible scuffle, and to Molly's horror, she heard the key card slide into the lock.

Instinctively she looked for somewhere to hide, but there was nowhere. Not even large enough furniture to crouch behind. Even the bed was too low to the ground.

The door opened.

She tried to close it again, but the larger of the two men stuck his foot in so she couldn't. "Excuse me. I'm not dressed." She tried to convey annoyance rather than the abject fear she had that two strangers were in her hotel room uninvited.

She slammed the door several times on his foot but he didn't show any expression. The smaller man looked apologetic. "Ms. Solent. I am so sorry for this inconvenience. I am Mr. Stelio, the hotel duty-manager. This is an investigator from the Russian embassy. It seems—"

"You were the last person to speak to Dr. Doubrov before his criminal assassination." The larger man interrupted in a deep voice with a thick accent, dragging out the word "criminal" like he was in a James Bond movie. "So. We need to talk, you and I. Correct?"

Fear spiked through her. The man pushed his way into the room and stood by the window, looking out over the city. The hotel manager hovered in front of the bathroom nervously wringing his hands.

Molly hitched her towel up as far as she could. She shoved her chin up. "If you wish to talk to me, you can make an appointment, and I will be dressed for it. You can't just barge—"

"I can do whatever I want to do, Ms. Solent. I am sure you wouldn't want to impede the investigation into the murder of a member of the Russian government, would you? Especially as you seemed to be so well acquainted?"

Oh my God. What did he know? "I have only met him at conferences. That is the extent of our acquaintance." Her cadence started to reflect the Russian's proper sentence construction. Funny thing was, if he hadn't pissed her off, she would probably have stuttered and stammered through an excuse, but anger superseded her nervousness.

He spun around to face her. "And yet I've heard from his security team that you held his hands for so very long before he was shot. Was it a signal? What did you say to him?"

A signal? "I said how nice it was to see him. I really didn't..." *have anything to do with his death... did I?*

"I think we should let Ms. Solent get dressed. Maybe you can make an appointment to speak to her further." Mr. Stelio shifted from one foot to another, obviously uncomfortable.

"Thank you—" Molly began.

"Absolutely out of the question," the Russian interrupted forcefully. "Time is everything in a murder investigation." He stepped much closer to Molly than was comfortable.

Her legs pressed against the bed but she had nowhere to go. She wasn't going to sit on the bed and allow him even greater physical power over her.

"I'm not sure you—either of you—understand the position you, and the whole of this country, are in. A member of the Russian Federation's government was brutally gunned down at a G20 meeting. In your country." He raised his eyes to the hotel manager.

"And with you"—looking back at Molly—"an American,

being the last person to talk to him." He slowly put his hands on his hips revealing a gun on his waist. "It really is in your best interests to cooperate with the investigation."

Molly's heart jumped a beat at the sight of his gun. She thought Europe had mostly banned guns. What had she gotten into? What were the messages about? What if he took her to the Russian embassy? No one would ever know where she was.

He stroked a thumb up and down the butt of the gun, as if he was contemplating taking it out and blowing a kneecap. "We saw you passing information. That is what his protection thinks. A thumb drive perhaps? Are you an agent for the United States of America? With your dark hair, you could easily be Chechen too. Let me tell you, our administration sees Chechen conspiracies faster than you sell antiquities. And the gulags are pleasant this time of year I hear. If...you survive the journey."

"Wait a minute. I did not sell antiquities—" but she kind of had. Or at least had unknowingly worked for a company that had sold antiquities that she and her boss had found. He must have really done his homework about her. While she was sleeping, he must have been digging up her past. The thought chilled her more. She tried to gather her thoughts. "I'm here to speak out against such practices. And while we are on the subject of dubious practices, I highly doubt my embassy would look kindly on you barging into my room, not even allowing me to dress, and interrogating me.

A movement in the door caught her eye. David muscled in behind the hotel manager, holding his cell phone up to video what was going on in the room. The Russian didn't see him. Thank God he'd found her. Her shoulders slumped in relief.

The Russian hissed at her in anger. "Your embassy, you foolish girl, will cooperate with my investigation lest our inquiries point at them. And if they don't, we will all know that the United States of America assassinated a member of Putin's government. Trust me when I say they won't want to go to war over this. They will give you up to us, regardless of what you did, or didn't do."

"And will your government give you up when this little movie I'm making hits YouTube? Of you storming a hotel room with a gun and victimizing an American woman who is only here to talk to the G20 countries about archaeology? With no authority?" David said, as if he was having a conversation about grabbing coffee.

That is until the Russian drew his gun.

"Give that phone to me immediately!" the Russian said, flicking a lever on the gun. Was that the safety? Was he really going to shoot David?

Molly's knees started to wobble, and the hotel manager disappeared into the corridor. She couldn't really blame him.

"This phone? This one? Okay. Oh, whoops. Look at that. Already uploaded. Right next to the video about a cat that loves water. Look. Aw. It's taking a bath in a kitchen sink." David showed the phone's screen to him and then laughed. "It really is so cute. Look, it has over a million views. Oh, do you think your video will beat that? It might go viral." His voice hardened. "That would be fun wouldn't it? Your career would be over. You are KGB right? Or SVR? A rose by any other name is as sweet though, don't you think? KGB, SVR it's all the same. Tell me, what are their disciplinary measures like? Same as they used to be? Shot by recruits?" He looked at the phone again and grinned. "Guess you'll find out soon."

She couldn't believe he was being so calm. But with his background in bomb disposal, she guessed he was used to being calm under pressure. Dammit, he was *so* cool.

The Russian holstered his weapon and cracked his neck. "Don't get in my way. I intend to solve this murder," he said, as he shouldered David out of his way. The air in the room left with him. As he slammed the door, Molly slumped to the bed.

"Thank God you came. He was threatening to take me to the gulag. That's probably as bad as it sounds right?" Her whole body was shaking uncontrollably. And she was cold.

David sat beside her and rubbed the small of her back, heating the blood rushing around there. "Didn't I tell you to stay put?" he asked mildly.

She leaned into him, needing his warmth, and his strength. And him. He'd rescued her again. He'd saved her the previous year when a maniac was holding a gun on her, he'd protected her the day before when someone was shooting, and he'd rescued her again just now from the gulag. Surely third time was the charm. Surely.

He disengaged from her and grabbed the desk chair, dragging it forward. "I was hoping it wouldn't come to this, but that"—he gestured to the door—"was nothing compared with what will happen if you don't leave. Everything he said was right. I'm not sure how far the embassy will go to protect you if the Russians press the point. If the US takes you in, well, the visuals of the US harboring a suspected assassin at a G20 conference…" He shook his head. "I just don't know how that will play out."

She flexed her fingers to combat the feeling that her hand muscles had frozen in place. Isn't that where rigor mortis started? Her head was shaking. How had this trip gone from something she'd been looking forward to for months to this level of calamity in just a few hours? "I'm not an assassin. Don't even say that. This whole thing is ridiculous."

He edged closer and took her hands in his, gradually returning the feeling to them. "It might be crazy, but this is where you are now. You have to leave. Today, if we can get you on a flight. I can't stay with you. I have a job here too."

Molly suddenly realized what he was saying. "You're leaving me? Again?"

"Strictly speaking, you'll be leaving me. We have about a couple of hours, maybe three, before he comes back with the Greek police and a warrant. You need to be gone by then." He sat back as if the matter had been settled.

"That's absolutely out of the question." Her voice rose, and she could feel the hysteria growing in her body. "It's not happening."

David looked stunned, but try as she might, she couldn't dial it back. She jumped up and rushed to the bathroom, slamming the door behind her. She braced herself on the vanity and took some breaths. Okay. This wasn't his fault. She was trying to blame someone other than herself.

She looked in the mirror and tried to gather her wits. How stupid could she have possibly been to agree to Brandon's plan? She wasn't a spy. She was terrible at that stuff. She was shit at lying, shit at hiding things…she wasn't exactly stellar at keeping secrets either. What had possessed her to get involved? Now a man was dead, and David thought she was a total idiot.

She'd ruined everything. This tour of speeches and conference was her way of atoning for the mess she'd found herself in last year. She'd spent her whole adult life working to preserve archaeological artifacts, only to find out that the company she'd done digs for was stealing the treasures from under everyone's noses. This speech here at the G20 was the culmination of her penance. This was the one that would get worldwide coverage. The grand finale. The one that she knew would make a difference. She wasn't sure if she could walk away from it. To go home and just go back to work as if none of it had mattered.

And she hated herself, really hated herself, that she was also pissed that David was leaving her again. He hadn't even flirted with her. Not so much as a look that might have had a double meaning. She was so stupid to have wasted a year on the mere hope of him. Someone she'd known had died, and here she was thinking about a man, for God's sake.

She sniffed back tears. She wished David wasn't outside the bathroom door. She'd give anything for a legitimate sobfest. But she had to man up and deal with what was going on. She stood up straight, and tried to look as dignified as she could in a hotel towel.

She opened the door and forced her chin up. "Okay, I'm sorry…"

He held his finger up. He was on the phone. "Yes sir. Yes. Of course, sir." He raised his eyebrows at her, and she shook her head.

It didn't matter. She just needed to get dressed and leave. Go home. Forget all this. She couldn't rely on anyone. Not Brandon, and not David. She had to take control of the situation. Regardless of how woefully inept she'd already proved herself to be. At that sliver of a negative thought, a wave of insecurity washed over her.

He was still on the phone with his back to her, nodding occasionally at whatever the person on the other end had said. She took a breath and just watched him in a way she'd never been able to before. His shirt was tight across his back, his waist was slim, and his jeans rode low. They were the type of jeans you wore when you weren't concerned with designer names, and they suited him perfectly. A little frayed around the edges, a little beaten up, but still functioning…and sexy. She gave a little smile when she realized she could have been describing David. Something twinged in her. God, she still wanted him so much. Wanted to love him. Wanted to see what he looked like when he was having sex. Climaxing.

Jesus…What she wanted to do is get a grip. She wrapped her towel firmly around her body and caught sight of herself in the floor length mirror outside the bathroom. She wanted to cry. Despite everything, how could this moment be any more convenient? She was almost naked, David was in the hotel room with her? And still he wasn't interested? Well that did it. She just had to admit how completely stupid she'd been this past year and move on.

"Roger that, sir. Nope, I'll pass Mal the message for you." He nodded another couple of times and then hung up.

"Are you almost ready to go?" he asked, barely offering her a look.

"Nope," she said, trying to tamp down her annoyance. "I'm staying. I don't care what happens to me, but I am giving this speech. I'm sorry that you got involved, and of course, thank you for helping me last night, but you should go now. Get on with your life, and let me get on with mine, at last." She twisted her finger in the air, telling him to turn around so that she could get dressed. Why she bothered doing that though, she had no idea. It was obvious he had no residual feelings for her.

Must not touch. Must not touch, he repeated to himself as he obediently looked out at the Greek government complex opposite. He heard her towel hit the floor, and his dick sprang uncomfortably to life in his jeans. He shifted from leg to leg, trying not to give in to it.

He wanted her more than he'd wanted anything in his life. But to keep her out of the hands of the Russian SVR he had to be thinking about their next move, not how lush her body looked, dewy from the shower. How sexy she looked with her chin shoved up, telling him to get on with his life. Her tan skin peeking out from the crisp white towel. The dreams he'd had about her all year. The vivid, tactile dreams that left him awake in the morning with a hard-on that propped up the sheets *and* the blankets on his bed. Every bad thought he'd had in the last year had been about her.

Even though they had never kissed. Even though he'd been mostly drunk the whole time he'd known her. Understandably so, but still. It was as though merely hugging her that last time they saw one another at the airport in Iraq—just that one embrace—had embedded her DNA so deeply in him all he could think about was her.

It took the will of a saint not to turn around and look. Touch. Taste. But something was off with Molly. Something she wasn't telling him. And he intended to get to the bottom of it, come hell or high water, before he succumbed to her. He could feel her pull, like attracting magnets. Dammit. He had to get his head back in the game.

He'd already made himself a target by coming into the hotel room. He could have let the Russian intelligence officer continue his interrogation, and kept his identity out of it, but, yeah. That hadn't really been an option.

When he saw the hotel manager standing by Molly's open hotel room, he suspected the worst. His whole world had almost collapsed in on him. She was dead. Whoever had killed the minister had come back for her. In the two seconds it had taken him to reach her doorway, he'd already imagined his life without the possibility of her in it. Trying to live knowing that she'd died on his watch. Wondering if he'd survive the crushing defeat his soul had felt. It wasn't anything he wanted to experience again. It wasn't anything he was going to let happen. Whatever happened now, he was staying with her. And his boss was going to kill him. Maybe even fire him. And given David's instinct to protect Molly rather than the man he was actually being paid to look after, he couldn't really blame him.

Distracted, he turned to tell her that he would stay with her. For as long as she was in danger. Big. Mistake. She was naked, sure. Phenomenally naked. But what struck him, made it impossible to turn away, was the worry on her face. Her eyes shone with unshed tears, the crease on her forehead spoke of worrying thoughts floating through her head.

"You don't have to worry. I'm not leaving you again." He hoped she couldn't hear how unsteady his words were.

She looked up, startled. Her instinct was to look for something to cover herself with, but there wasn't anything within reach. He wanted to do the honorable thing. To turn around and give her the privacy she asked for. But he couldn't. He took a step toward her, never taking his eyes from hers.

Her lips trembled beneath his gaze, and she held up her hand to stop him. He stopped in his tracks.

"You promised to come find me, but it felt like you were promising more." Her voice wavered as she attempted to cross her arms over her breasts. He tried to keep his eyes on her face.

There was no way he could lie to her, not with her standing there, naked and vulnerable.

"I did promise"—he paused—"but I probably was in no shape to promise anything." And now he wanted to promise her everything, but still wasn't sure if he should. "I'm sorry. I should have called. Written. But it never felt like the right time..." *I didn't want to hurt you. I've never deserved you.*

"Did you think about me?" she asked softly.

His dick was heavy and hot in his pants. He didn't answer her immediately, wondering if he should admit to his weakness. He was trying to control this dynamite, trying to get some control over the room again, when every part of his brain wanted to lose itself in her.

"Every day. I..."—He stopped himself going too far. Past the point of no return—"Every day."

Her crossed arms dropped, as well as her gaze. His body started working without permission.

He couldn't even put up a token resistance. An honorable one. Honor was already in his rearview mirror.

He tugged his T-shirt over his head and slowly went to her. Slowly so he could marvel at her, the sudden light in her eyes.

He was far from certain. About what he wanted from her, about the wisdom of getting entangled—because he had no doubt that is exactly what he was doing. With every step he was getting irrevocably entangled in Molly.

He stopped a few inches short of her glorious nakedness. The briefest flicker of a frown danced across her forehead. He took a breath and with both hands, pulled her against him, fast and hard. As she gasped, he claimed her mouth with a ferocity that startled him. For a second. And then he was drowning. He'd fantasized about the taste of Molly. Now it was all his. All fucking his. And so was she.

Her hands ran through his short hair, and one settled on his neck as she let him bend her backward with his need to consume her. Her other hand splayed against his chest. Blood pumped through him like he was in combat. Throbbing heat flooded over him, and instinct took over.

Yes!

There was a second of triumph and relief when he'd admitted to thinking about her every day. When she realized for absolute sure that he wanted her as much as she wanted him. At *freaking* last. The tension of being so close to him, but not actually being close to him, evaporated, and all her birthdays and Christmases arrived at once. David. Holding her. Kissing her with the fierceness with which a warrior stalks his prey. He felt out of control to her. She loved it, and was scared by it.

She felt brazen and vulnerable at the same time—her nakedness pressed against his half-clothed body—and more like a woman than she ever had before.

"Are you sure?" his voice rasped against her throat, sending shivers of excitement through her. She couldn't find the words to reassure him, so she traced her fingers down his arm, and drew his hand between her legs.

A groan rumbled through his body when he felt how wet she was for him, as she had been ever since she'd woken up in the same hotel room as him, desperate for his touch. She wanted to do a victory lap. This was really happening.

He stroked along her wetness, virtually trembling against her as he felt his way around her. Her breath mirrored his, unsteady as he circled her clitoris slowly, deliberately. Her head dropped back, limp with the waves of pleasure both physical and mental. Electricity fritzed in her lower back as he stroked her steadily and firmly.

He pulled his hand away, and she moaned, opening her eyes. He gazed at her for a second, and pulled her upright and put his hands on her shoulders. "You deserve all the promises in the world. I'm just not there yet. I'm—"

She laid her fingers against his lips. "Shhh. I'm not asking for any promises. I'm not asking for tomorrow. I'm not making that mistake again. I'm not asking for your soul, either." She frowned. "I just want now. This second. I just want *you*."

He held her gaze for a couple of seconds, as if measuring her sincerity. And then he dropped his head. "I don't des—"

"Don't say that. You might get to choose what you deserve. But I do too. I deserve this." She wanted to stamp her foot. "I deserve you. I waited so long. Thought about you for so long. Said 'no' to so many dates. You *ruined* this past year for me. So the way I see it, you owe me now."

He raised his head with the beginnings of a smile playing around the corners of his mouth. "I owe you, huh?" He narrowed his eyes and walked her backward until her calves hit the bed.

"Yes you do," she replied in a whisper. "And I intend on collecting." She put her hands on the front of his pants, as if she was going to undo them. But instead she stroked down and fluttered her fingers over his dick, which felt hard and strong under the denim. Her whole body reacted to the anticipation of having him fill her. Own her. Complete her.

He let her stroke him through his pants for a few seconds, but when she could tell he needed more, she undid his button and slowly drew down the zip. As tight against the bed as she was, she had to sit on the end to drag them off his hips. His dick sprang free and she closed her eyes briefly in reverence. She couldn't believe that she was here, after all this time.

She blew lightly on his dick, causing him to sway backward a little. He probably expected her to tease him a little, so instead she opened her mouth and placed it around him in one swift motion so that he would feel her tongue, the heat of her mouth, and the tightness all in one sensation.

"Jesus," he hissed between his teeth, as she sucked the length of him between her lips. She stroked his balls as she released him, sucking briefly again on the tip.

In a single movement, he lifted her up until she was standing and kicked off his pants. The tip of his dick fit perfectly between her legs as they stood. Purposefully she shuffled forward so that she could clasp her thighs around him.

He withdrew from her and bent to claim a nipple. He bit until she gasped, making the hard nub ache for more. Threads of desire rushed from her breasts to between her legs, a heavy wetness settling there, waiting for him.

She moaned and couldn't help but squeeze her other nipple in tandem. He pulled away and watched her hand for a second before gently kicking her feet apart until she was standing with her legs wide open. He stood back, his dick dancing upright, begging to be touched, but he wouldn't let her.

Instead he very deliberately looked at her pussy, watching as he slid his hand over her mound. His intent gaze turned her on so much, she felt light-headed. He pushed her so she was sitting again on the end of the bed. Her legs were still wide open, and he knelt between them.

"You're beautiful down here. Pink, luscious..." his words trailed off as he used two fingers to open her folds. He licked her clitoris firmly, then pulled away to look at her face.

"Do you like touching yourself?" he asked hoarsely.

"Sometimes," she whispered, as he placed a finger at her entrance.

"When do you touch yourself?" He slowly started to slide one finger inside her up to his knuckle.

She whimpered.

He pulled his finger out, and paused. "When do you touch yourself?" he repeated.

"When I'm alone," she said. "When I'm in the shower. When I'm thinking about you." It was true, and she felt brave and sexy telling him. Saying the words out loud.

He slid two fingers into her, and her head fell back in submission to the waves of need pulsing through her. "When you're touching yourself, what do you imagine I'm doing to you?" He reached down again and started tonguing her clit again. Heat spiked through her spine.

"I'm going to come!" she said, surrendering her body to the familiar tipping point.

But he stopped. "No, you can't come until you've told me what I'm doing to you when you're masturbating. I want to know."

Desperate for her release, desperate to have him inside her, she gave in. "I close my eyes and think of passing you in the street. We look at each other but don't say anything. You push me into an alley and hitch up my skirt so if anyone was walking by, they'd see us, and you'd shove your hand in my panties and stroke me until I came."

"I can do that. Do you like the idea of being caught, of being watched?" He stood, knelt on the bed, picking her up and laying her on the bed.

"Yes," she choked out, almost but not quite embarrassed. If she was going to give herself to David, for one night, or two, or maybe forever, she may as well expose herself totally to him.

He wrapped his hand around her neck in such a way that it was almost dangerous, almost brutal. He kissed her hard on the mouth, his tongue dominating hers, but she felt only desire for him. Already, this was so much better than her fantasies.

She opened her legs, begging for his touch, and he slipped his hand there as if it had belonged there their whole lives. It probably had.

He stroked her, using her lubrication to dance his fingers around her clit, and smooth across her ass. He pressed for admittance, and she returned the pressure. He seemed to laugh to himself a little as he moved back to her clit.

"The good thing is, I like watching." He ran a finger around one of her nipples.

But she couldn't take that much more. "Please. Please I want you so badly, David. I need you inside me. I've waited..."

At her words, his dick elevated even farther. "Your wish..." he said, grabbing his pants and taking out a condom.

He knelt again between her legs and drew her thighs over his. He rested his dick at her entrance. "You know what's good about this? I get to watch you take my dick inside you." He pressed against her until she felt the tip of him inside her. "I get to watch your pussy open for me, your clit beg for me."

At his forceful words, she nearly came, attaining a plateau of need higher than she'd ever felt before.

He kneeled up and started thrusting inside her, hard, fast. It hurt, but in an amazing way. With every thrust he groaned as if she were bringing him to life. She watched the expression on his face change into one of blind, out-of-control need. Seeing her look at him, he licked his finger and pressed against her clitoris, dragging it with every thrust.

Heat splayed across her belly and up to her breasts, and she instinctively cupped them in her hands. As he thrust, his gaze rested on her hands. *He liked to watch, did he?* As excitement took her conscious movements, she removed her hands, except for her fingers. She played with her own nipples, pinching and twisting them, igniting a blaze of fire that jagged into her, taking her to her climax. The pressure on her clit increased with his thrusts and exploded in her spine, causing her to groan as it pulsed through her.

David took two more thrusts and groaned, "Molly," as he closed his eyes and tipped his head down, taking heavy breaths.

Sweet Jesus. She never imagined it would be like that. How could she let him go now, knowing that he could do that to her? Knowing he could lift her to a level of need she'd never, ever felt.

She closed her eyes and took a deep breath. She felt his fingers lightly stroking her sides, almost tickling. His touch flickered over her nipples again, puckering them again.

"You're so beautiful. And you have a filthy mind," David said smiling. "I love that." His fingers drifted south until they were touching her clit again, so lightly. She took a jagged breath as he held the condom on as he withdrew from her.

He went to the bathroom and suddenly she felt vulnerable. Was that it? Was it once and done for him? What was she thinking about? She'd told him that this was all she wanted. But that was before... She should have kept her mouth shut.

Molly. Get a grip. He's said that he's not reliable, or at least not ready yet. She looked for the edge of the sheet so she could cover herself.

David emerged almost immediately and paused. "Don't hide yourself from me. I want to see you. All of you. Always."

Always? Maybe this *wasn't* over for him. She pulled back the sheet and lay back down.

He lay on top of the bed next to her and swung over onto one elbow. "I fantasized too. But it didn't come close to the reality of touching you." His hand tracked down her side to her hip. "Of fucking you."

Her breath hitched, and he smiled a very smug, confident smile. He was a god in bed. It was like he knew everything about her, every place to touch her, everything that would get a response from her. He dragged her against him and draped a leg over hers.

She closed her eyes, satiated, safe, and protected.

After about ten minutes, Molly moved. She couldn't bear to be still. Crazy because she'd been dreaming of post-sex euphoria with David for months. And she wanted to stay wrapped in his arms, basking in the wickedness he'd brought out in her. But she was also antsy. Restless. The visit from the Russian had shaken her, and all she really wanted to do was switch on the television and see CNN announcing that the authorities had caught the person responsible for Dr. Doubrov's death.

She rolled over the bed and reached for the remote and proceeded to punch the buttons until the familiar CNN logo showed up. What she saw made her bolt upright. Rolling text on the screen below footage of a burning storefront said, "Anarchists cause mayhem in Greek capital with G20 leaders' meeting just weeks away. Russians blame America for assassination of Minister Doubrov." Her heart started racing as she tried to figure out what it meant.

"David. Look." She hit his leg, eyes still on the rolling text of doom.

"I see it." He was already sitting up next to her, and she hadn't noticed. They listened to the CNN anchor's measured tones explaining that the burning store was a Russian business, and that Moscow had insisted that Athens close down until the authorities found those responsible for what they called "a western-sponsored attack on the people of Russia."

Molly whimpered. Literally a whimper came out of her mouth. She stretched her fingers out, trying to get rid of the numb coldness that had settled there in the previous few minutes. They shook.

David wrapped a warm arm around her and tucked the duvet around her. "Stay there. Keep warm and let me make a few phone calls." His calm, low voice reassured her.

Slightly.

David stepped out on to his small balcony and called Mal, because who else? He seemed to always have his ear to the scuttlebutt, no matter where it came from. He called it bullshit filtering.

"S'up." Mal answered with.

"I just saw the news. Is Russia stirring the pot, or is..."

"Is your country actually plotting the downfall of Russia?"

David used a visualizing technique he learned in therapy and imagined himself kicking Mal shitless.

"I just want to know what's going on, buddy, okay?" He tried and failed to reach for a measured tone.

"Right you are. Touchy lot, you Yanks. Okay, so *all* I've heard is that the good old US of A is actually waging a covert war against Russia. Literally everyone from any country in the know"—he meant in the espionage business—"says all the chatter points to the CIA."

"Shit." David couldn't get his head around that. It was so…uncharacteristic. No one used their intelligence agencies to take down a country.

"Well, shit, or maybe bullshit."

"What do you mean?" David felt a glimmer of hope.

"Everyone had heard the same thing, but no one could tell me who the intel came from with any degree of confidence. Even the hot Russian chick. And I *really* tried to persuade her to tell. Chatter, nothing firm."

"So…smoke and mirrors?"

"Mate. I know you think it's good that it might not be true. And it is. But that makes it exponentially worse for you and your girl. If this is a war of misinformation, you two are on the front lines. Not to mention *really* easy targets.

David paused. He was right. If his country was really on the warpath, and frankly, most Americans would be totally behind unseating Putin and restoring glasnost to Russia, Molly and David needed to leave. And if this *was* all smoke and mirrors, and someone was setting the US up to take the fall for the assassination and the bombing, then they needed to get the fuck out of dodge too. "Bottom line is we're leaving."

Mal paused. "That's a good idea. I've been reassigned, and I told Baston about you and Molly. Expect a phone call."

Baston was the owner and operator of Barracks Security. The man who had given David his second chance. That settled it. He couldn't go against Baston's wishes, and he wasn't going to leave Molly. So they were out of here.

Mal must have taken his silence for anger because he continued, "Don't look at me like that"—David looked at his phone and rolled his eyes—"I can't be your babysitter if I'm not in the same country as you."

"Babysitter, my ass." David clenched his fist.

"Enabler maybe. Anyway, got to run. Stay safe, brother."

"You too." The line went dead before he'd finished the last word.

Tosser. David half-smiled at himself already using Mal's favorite epithet.

He let himself back in the room and explained to Molly that they had to leave for the airport. She seemed to have gone from shaking to icy-cold determination in the time he was out on the balcony.

"Not even remotely acceptable," she said, even though ten minutes ago she'd been terrified. "I have a speech to give, and I'm not missing it. It's important to me, and important that the world hears what happened last year and the implications of artifact trafficking." She shoved her chin up in an adorable dare-to-tell-me-I'm-wrong way.

He hesitated. He wanted to exert his authority. Tell her there was no way they could make her speech, that they had to leave. But he couldn't. He couldn't deny her this…catharsis. Not least because he had been a part of the trafficking last year. "What time is the speech?"

"At five p.m. There are no questions, it should be just an hour." She said, getting out of bed, still naked, and completely, blissfully unembarrassed. She was like walking, fucking, sex. He felt a twitch again. She turned to her suitcase and bent over to extract some items. No way could he ignore that.

In a second he was behind her, cupping her breast and lightly pinching her nipple. Her moan was like nutrition feeding his need for her.

She stood upright, her body flush against his as he reached around and cupped the other breast too. A perfect fucking handful. How was he going to walk away from her?

She wriggled against him, and his dick hardened between her ass cheeks. He pinched her nipples harder, reveling in the feel beneath his fingers and the groan that vibrated through her. He nudged her legs apart and, with a hand between her shoulders, he pushed her forward until she was braced against the wall with both arms outstretched and legs open to him.

He stepped back just to get a visual to remember. She was fucking glorious. Dropping to one knee, eye level with her pussy, he drew his finger lightly over her ass, all the way to her clitoris, just loving the sight and feel of her.

She wriggled, taking a tiny step back so his mouth was close to her. He blew on her exposed hot flesh, and she gasped. Then he flicked his tongue lightly on her clit while slowly sliding his fingers inside her. He stroked her with his tongue in time with his stroking fingers inside her until she gasped and spasmed, allowing him to feel and taste her orgasm. She was on fire. She came so easily for him, it was like an instant aphrodisiac.

He stood, and she immediately reached behind her for his dick, making him step closer to her. She stroked it once, and twice before directing it to her opening. He paused just long enough to fumble a condom, before pushing her forward again and pushing into her with one stroke.

"I love feeling you inside me," she said, in a part-groan. "Take me. Really take me."

He held on to her hips and pulled her back onto his dick. He felt like he was ramming her into the wall, but she moaned, "yes, yes." As each stroke took her further.

"Wait," she said suddenly.

He paused mid-stroke and felt his dick pulse in objection. "Am I hurting you?" He started to withdraw, but she shuffled back.

"Don't you dare. Stay right where you are," she ordered.

"Yes ma'am," was all he could say in reply.

She inexplicably rummaged in her suitcase, unzipping a pocket. She straightened a little and immediately he felt a vibration around his dick.

A vibrator? If it was even possible, he got harder. He could feel the vibration in his balls as he continued to fuck her. She held the toy half against her clit and half at her vagina. He felt every vibration and every twitch her body made in response.

He was going to last about three minutes...if that.

Her breath started coming in pants as he thrust into her, hard and deep. She came with an audible breath and a shudder.

He closed his eyes and emptied himself into her, the spasm of her own orgasm sucking every last bit of him into her.

As they stood there for a minute, he wondered how he was going to live the rest of his life knowing that Molly was in the world without him. Could he cope with the thought that she might be giving herself to someone else like this? Could he say goodbye? He was even reluctant to disengage from her, but he did, slowly, holding the condom in place.

She turned and laid her head on his chest and he stroked her hair. "You're really quite something, you know?"

She breathed a laugh against his chest. "Men usually say that before storming out of a date or dumping me," she said.

He squeezed her. "I don't believe either of those things have ever happened." He held her away from him before she could reply, because he really didn't want to get into the previous boyfriend territory. That way madness lay. "Anyway, shower time." He spun her and slapped her lightly on the ass.

She jumped toward the bathroom and looked back, raising an eyebrow at him as she disappeared into the shower.

He wished he'd gone to see her last year. Maybe he could have gotten her out of his system back then? He shook his head. No way. Out of everyone in the whole word, Molly would be the one who'd have totally messed with his system and broken him for anyone else.

Except he was already broken. Broken and not easily fixed.

CHAPTER FOUR

She was already clean by the time he joined her in the shower. He opened the glass door and stepped inside.

"How dirty are you?" he asked picking up the soap and lathering it.

"Very, very dirty," she said, straight-faced.

"You certainly look it." He stroked his soapy hands around her neck, massaged her shoulders a little, and then very thoroughly washed her breasts. God, she was in heaven with him. He was just so responsive to her physically. Her previous boyfriends had been academics. And she'd thought she liked that. Men who appreciated her for her mind and her experience, and recently, she assumed, because she'd been temporarily famous. But David. He responded to her on such a fundamental level, almost at a cellular level. And she reveled in his intensity, both physical and mental.

Mostly physical at that moment though. Her breasts were

super clean, and she stood with her eyes closed, just allowing the sensation of his hands to dominate the space around her. She was completely sated by her time with him, but Jesus…he slipped his hand between her legs, stroking with the lather, every inch.

She wriggled away with a laugh. "I need a rest. Wine. Coffee at the very least." She needed time to think about what she'd done. Of course, she'd wanted this all along. Of course she had, for virtually a whole year. But in her fantasies, he'd been complete. Confident and easy. But anyone with half a cell of perception could see that he was confident, but difficult to read, and maybe even broken. She could see uncertainty in his eyes when he looked at her. She was worried. There, she'd admitted it. She didn't want to get emotionally attached to him if he would just run away again. She had to keep her feelings in check. Sex, not emotion.

He turned off the water and handed her a towel from a rack. She grabbed it and wrapped herself up in it again, flashing back to when she took the decision to drop it on the floor. Now she wondered if she'd done the right thing.

She changed into a sundress, still crumpled from her luggage. The heat and humidity would ease out the wrinkles in no time at all.

David came out of the shower and got straight on the phone after kissing her bare shoulder. "Hey Mal, have you checked out yet? Good, we're coming down."

He put his phone down and pulled on his clothes from earlier. "Mal's leaving, and if we go now, we can stay in his room until we're ready to go. No one here knows that we were here together, so if anyone comes looking for you or me, they won't find us."

A finger of fear poked her stomach as she suddenly remembered her predicament. She nodded and looked around the room anxiously. "We should probably go now, shouldn't we?" Suddenly being where the Russian agent had threatened them with a gun sent chills down her spine.

"I'm ready if you are," he said evenly. "We're going down to the fourth floor via my room." He held his arm out and she slid under it. He squeezed her once, and tension seeped out of her like water from a sponge. She was protected. Safe.

They arrived at Mal's room as he was leaving. He was a big man with features to match. At around six and a half feet, he towered over Molly and was just a little taller than David. Dark stubble speckled his face, and only his clear blue eyes showed any expression. He bumped fists with David and handed him a key.

"Be careful of him," he said to Molly. "We've only just put him back together."

"Fuck off," David said evenly.

"Love you too, mate," he replied cracking a smile. "Don't die. I don't want to arse around training someone else." Mal picked up his bag and headed down the corridor.

"What training?" David said loudly, grinning at his retreating back.

Mal just raised a hand without turning around and disappeared around the corner.

Clearly he hadn't planned on waiting for them. Molly was glad they'd gotten there in time to get his key card.

"Hi guys!" a chirpy voice came from the other end of the corridor. It was Victoria.

"Hi! What have you been doing?" Molly asked, as she leaned into the rather exuberant hug that Victoria offered.

"Obviously nothing as fun as you," she said with a sly smile. She held her hand out to David. "Victoria Ruskin, WAMP. The voice of the tri-cities."

"Nice to meet you, Victoria. I'm David," he said, wondering which tri-cities she was talking about.

"Do you two fancy having lunch? I found a great place away from the madness here. I've heard some crazy gossip about what went down last night."

Molly glanced at David, who looked interested. "Sure, that would be great. Can we meet you there? We have a little unpacking to do first."

"Awesome. It's on the corner of Sina and Skoufa behind the hotel a few blocks. Great souvlaki, fabulous mimosas. Say in an hour?"

"Sure, see you there!" Molly said.

They opened Mal's door and marveled for a moment at the array of empty bottles he'd left in there. Kristal champagne, which Molly remembered was being served at the cocktail party, and a variety of beers.

"It's amazing he can function," David said, shaking his head. "He didn't tell anyone he was checking out early, so let's just put our bags in the closet and call for housekeeping."

Molly didn't say anything, just wondered if Mal was in the same place as David had been. As if he'd read her mind he said,

"I know it looks like he has a problem, but he doesn't. He's just English. Mostly everyone I've met from there can drink like it's a national skill-set."

At Molly's silence, David turned. He noticed her dress for the first time. Really noticed it. Her sundress was a pale yellow with thin straps, and, God help him, with the light of the window behind her, it was almost transparent. Her hair, almost the same color as her dress, was still damp and curled around her face. She was mesmerizing.

She smiled. "We have an hour. Do you actually want to unpack, or get out of the hotel?"

"What do you suggest?" He really wanted to stay in the room with her and demand she remove her dress so he could see her naked again. He was fairly sure that she had only the tiniest panties and no other underwear on. He swore he could virtually see her nipples through the dress. If he looked really hard. Really hard.

Jesus, man. Get a fucking grip.

"There is the Temple of Olympian Zeus just around the corner. We could take a walk there. It was the largest temple in Athens when they built it."

"Sure. Sounds like a plan."

As they made their way out of the hotel, David couldn't figure out if people were staring at them because Molly was a total knockout, or because they'd already been fingered as suspects. Whichever it was, it was making him feel uncomfortable. He didn't like people noticing him.

They walked toward the temple, David wanting to poke

the eyes out of any man who looked at her. This was not a natural reaction, he was sure. He needed to bring things back on track.

"What do you know about this Doubrov guy?" he asked. "Was he into anything he shouldn't have been?"

Molly was silent for a beat too long. "Not that I know of. I really didn't know him that well at all. We were on the same archaeological conference circuit, but I really only knew him from attending his lectures, and the meet and greets afterward. He'd just passed a message through my boss that he was looking forward to seeing me again."

"What exactly did you say to him when you met him at the party? In fact, why were you at the party with jeans and sneakers on?"

"The airline lost my bag with my cocktail dress in it," she said as she pointed across the road to the tops of the temple pillars.

He noticed that she hadn't answered his first question and a cloud of concern—or was it suspicion?—bloomed in his stomach. He took her hand to cross the road, wanting to make sure she couldn't run. And suddenly he wondered why he thought she would. Instinct? He hadn't been able to rely on his instinct for a few years. He wasn't sure he could now. "And you couldn't have waited for the cocktail party the next evening, or the evening after that?"

"Well, I had my speech tomorrow, and I was supposed to have a few days to relax afterward, maybe visit an old dig or two, but I guess that's out of the question now, right?" She pulled some tickets out of her purse and handed them to a woman in the box, who gave her two brochures with color photos of the temple.

The temple loomed in front of them, huge white columns against a dark blue sky. It was a beautiful ruin, he had to admit. But it didn't diminish the feeling that he was missing something key. Something he should have remembered. It chilled him that he wasn't on top of his game, and he wondered if it was Molly fucking him up, or his own special demons doing the job.

As they walked around the site, he thought for the first time since he'd hit Athens about his EOD brother Danny, who had died in an explosion when he'd playfully kicked a soccer ball, on patrol in Afghanistan. A ball that had been filled with explosives. It had been nearly a decade ago, but as his therapist pointed out over and over, seeing the explosion, feeling the blast, smelling the burned flesh was *not* normal. Remembering it was normal. Being horrified by that memory was normal. His life however, was not normal, and at this stage he didn't even know what normal looked like.

She sat on a bench facing the ruins. "I like to imagine the people who lived here, who worshipped here."

He sat beside her and put his arm around her like they were teenagers on a park bench. Embarrassed he drew it back again, but she grabbed his hand and snuggled in his shoulder, despite the heat of the day. She fit there.

He took a breath, and then another. He wanted to just enjoy this today, because tonight they would both be gone and this would be a memory. Even if she wouldn't tell him exactly what was going on, after today he didn't really need to know her secrets. And would probably be better off not knowing them.

A man in a suit entered the site. He didn't stop at the ticket booth, he just showed the lady something. David stood up. "Is there another way out of here?"

"Only over there." She pointed to the other side of the temple, close to the way they'd come in.

David made a fairly simple deduction. The man was in a suit, so he wasn't a tourist. He didn't buy a ticket, so he probably flashed a badge or some kind of ID at the ticket woman. And, he and Molly were virtually the only people there.

"Molly, listen to me. I think that man is either with the police, or something worse. I'm going to distract him while you get to the exit. Go meet Victoria for lunch and I'll meet you there, you remember where she said?"

"Sure. Sina and Skoufa." Molly gathered her purse and looked anxiously at the exit.

"Great. Order me a doner kebab will you? I'll be right behind you." He caught her hand as she made to move and kissed it, trying to alleviate the concern etched on her face. The same concern that he felt.

She gave him a quick smile and headed in the opposite direction around the temple.

He coughed loudly to make the man look at him. It worked. Their eyes met and the other man's step faltered a little. Excellent.

"Hi there," he said lifting his hand and flashing a wide, wide smile. "How ya doin'?"

The man slowed right down and looked behind him in confusion. By the time he looked back, David was right on top of him. He stopped walking.

"Whatcha doin' here? Looking at the temple? It's quite somethin' isn't it?" He played a Deep South accent, cowboy-type. The type people expect to find in an American abroad.

The man up close was clearly out of place, pale, thinning hair, badly fitting suit. There was not much he could do to cover what he was doing. He was a dud in a suit at a tourist site. He knew he was busted.

"Who are you here for? Me, or the family over there?"

"Excuse me," he replied in accented English as he tried to brush past David.

David just turned and walked with him. "Did your buddy tell you that I videoed him interrogating an American citizen without allowing her any legal recourse? That was so cool. Look, I can show you the footage. It was awesome. He took out his gun and everything. Just like an old school KGB officer. You know, Cold War days."

The man stopped and looked closer at David, and then at the phone he was holding up. He shrugged. "You know it's not so much cold war anymore. These days it's an arctic freeze. And you don't want to be in the middle of that. The exposure could kill you."

David couldn't believe his ears. "You're in Greece, buddy. That's in the European Union. Ally of the USA. You're not going to be able to ride roughshod over the authorities here."

"And you, 'buddy' should read a newspaper every so often. Greece is considering breaking with the EU and looking to its old World War II ally, Russia, for a bailout. And when we seal the deal with the new government"—he lowered his voice into a whisper—"we'll have Russian military bases in a NATO country. Oh the fun we will have with you then."

Jesus, he really did need to read a newspaper. He knew things were up in the air with the Greek government and the EU, but not *that* far up in the air. "You're talking EU politics here, and we're American. If you make a move on her—for any convoluted reason—I will ensure you will pay. You personally." He dipped his head. "Okay, maybe also your friend."

The man sighed and shook his head wearily. "I don't care. I've been doing this for nearly thirty years. I do what I'm told when I'm told to do it. I don't make waves, and I'm not about to start now. But let me tell you this. There are things in play here that even I don't know. High level. I've been told that you are waging a war against my country." He shrugged. "That means we're following you, and following the girl. Beyond that I don't know."

Following the girl? David suddenly chilled in the hot air and turned his gaze toward the direction he'd sent her in. *Shit.*

He turned back to the Russian. "I didn't post that video of your colleague, you know."

"I do know that. There is an honor among thieves, and sometimes an honor among spies. It is for that professional courtesy, I tell you this about the girl so you can do whatever you need to do. Me? I'm here for the temple. It is a beauty."

David looked at him for a couple of seconds. Who would

have thought? "Enjoy it. Here." He shoved the brochure into his hand. "Thank you."

"Spasibo." The man nodded and turned away.

David ran for Molly. He hoped he hadn't sent her into harm's way.

CHAPTER FIVE

Molly walked past the ticket seller again and back toward the hotel. As much as she wanted to, she didn't look back. She was sure that David could handle himself, but still a finger of fear jabbed at her resolve to be a big girl. As she cleared the site, she ran across the two-lane road again and slipped down a small pedestrian street.

She pulled out her cell phone to try calling Brandon again. This whole "serve your country" thing was so far out of control now. There was no reply.

She took a chance and dialed the telephone number that was one digit away from Brandon's. A woman picked up.

"State Department, Brandon Peterson's office." The voice sounded tinny in the city air.

"I'd like to speak to Mr. Peterson please." Molly was relieved to be actually through to his office. Maybe he could fix all this. She ducked into a store and stuffed her finger in her other ear so she could hear better.

"I'm sorry, Mr. Peterson is out of the country. Can I take a message?"

Damn. Damn.

"Can you tell me when he'll be back?" she asked, hope dying with every word.

"I'm afraid not. Who is this please?" This time it was more of an indignant command. Molly pictured her with her hair in a bun, glasses perched on her nose, pressing some kind of CRAZY PERSON alarm button on her pristine desk. "Who is this?" Even more insistent. Almost panicked.

Was that an appropriate reaction to a caller for a man who was just out of the country?

Exasperated, and a little worried, she hung up.

She looked up at the road name and tried to figure out where the restaurant was. Checking her watch, she realized that Victoria probably wasn't even there yet, so she slowed down. Her head wasn't really into window-shopping, but she took her time looking as she went. She was about to walk past an artisan who made worry beads in his shop, but she stopped and went in. Worry beads would be a perfect gift for David. Help organize his worries, or fears, or prayers. She had no idea which one he'd choose to measure, and that made her simultaneously realize that she knew nothing about him.

She chose a set of matte black beads and made her way to their lunch appointment. If memory served, the restaurant should be just around the corner.

As she was about to cross the road, a man in a suit came out of a side road in front of her, walking quickly in the same direction she was. She instinctively slowed down. He looked to be the same height as the man who'd burst into her hotel room, the man David had thought was Russian SVR. So few men were in gray suits, and he stuck out like a sore thumb. As he rushed around the corner, his suit jacket flipped up, and she caught a glimpse of the gun he'd shown her earlier. She stopped in her tracks and watched him cross the road toward their lunch venue.

Looking around to make sure no one was following her, she ducked into a food store. How did he know they were going to that restaurant? Was David going to walk into some kind of ambush? She crouched down in the store, not really caring what she looked like to the people inside. What she really wanted to do is to curl up in a ball and rock. Rock herself back to the Lincoln Memorial, where she could say, "Hell, no!" to Brandon fucking Peterson.

She peeked out to see him look at his watch and scan the outside tables. Then he went inside, and Molly ran out of the store and pressed herself against the side of the building trying to figure out what to do. She didn't have Victoria's phone number, and frankly, excusing herself from the lunch date was fairly low on her priority list at that moment. Below "finding David" and "getting the hell out of Dodge."

She felt someone brush up against her and she jumped, spinning around, expecting the worst.

Thank God. David leaned up against the wall next to her. "Not hungry?"

Her hand searched for his. "The Russian guy from this morning just walked into the restaurant."

David said nothing, but eased her back from the corner and looked around it himself.

"He's not eating. He's standing over Victoria." He eased back around.

"Oh God, we have no way of warning her," Molly said, flashing back to his intimidating presence in her room that morning.

"She's an American reporter. If he tried anything, she'll have the story of her life. Don't worry, she'll be fine. Let's see what happens."

They watched the restaurant for a few minutes before a car drew up outside. Before it had even applied its parking brake, the man exited and got into the back of the car without breaking stride. "Phew," Molly said.

"Are you ready for lunch then? I'm starving," David said, as if he hadn't just escaped an interrogation or worse.

Molly's knees were warm and loose in the way they get when she was drunk, or scared witless. "You still want to go eat?"

"Sure. This is your day off, right? Let's go have lunch with your friend. We can ask her what the Russian wanted with her." He held his hand out to her, and she took it, sliding her hand slowly into his. Safe.

Victoria jumped up when they entered. "You came. I was getting worried."

David looked at his watch. They were only a few minutes late. He pulled out a chair for Molly, and then moved around and pushed Victoria's in too before taking his place. He intercepted an appreciative look that passed between them. Yup. He was the king of smooth.

He picked up the menu and pretended to read. Trying to position his query as casual chit-chat, he asked, "Who was that man you were talking to just before we walked in?"

Victoria looked startled and looked at the door. Then her face relaxed as if she understood the question. "I wasn't talking to anyone. A man came in and asked me if I'd seen any other Americans at the restaurant. Which was weird, since I was quite obviously the only person in here." She frowned. "Why?"

"No reason. I just thought I recognized him as he left. Had you seen him before?"

Her eyes shifted left briefly, and then met his. "No. Never seen him before." Victoria switched her attention to Molly. "Are you hungry? I recommend the souvlaki. It's awesome here."

Molly smiled, and seemed to relax into her chair. "Sounds great. I'll have that."

They ordered, and then Molly brought up the previous night. "Were you at the cocktail party last night, or did you go to your reporter place? Did you hear what happened?"

Victoria's eyes lit up, which, David guessed, would be the normal reaction to an assassination story. "I wasn't, I was at the Media Club. You know, one cocktail party looks very much like the other, especially when you come from DC, so I skipped it. And it turned out to be the only time I really wish I'd accepted the invitation. What happened? Did you see it? I'm pissed that I only got to see the coverage the next morning on CNN. So was my boss." She took a swig of her soda.

Molly caught David's eye, and he subtly shook his head at her. "No…well I mean, yes, I was there. But I didn't see anything. Just a crash and people running everywhere. And then this morning I heard that a Russian man had been killed." She leaned forward. "What have you heard? You said you had some gossip?"

Victoria paused, looking at Molly as if sizing her up for some kind of interview, and then semi-shrugged. "I haven't really heard anything definite other than what the police said last night. The man who was killed was a member of the Russian delegation, and there was no evidence left of the shooter because they'd rigged bombs to destroy everything they left. So strange, really. Who would want to assassinate a minister of antiquities?" She stared off into the distance for a second and then snapped her attention back to Molly. "What the grapevine says though is much less pretty." She glanced at both of them.

Molly's heartrate accelerated. "Yes?" she said lightly, feeling for David's knee under the table.

"I've heard rumors—and that's all they are for now—that the US is starting some kind of war against Russia. Not troops and tanks, yet, I guess, but by stealth. The assassination is just the beginning I hear." By the time she had finished, her voice had become a whisper, and she had all but ducked in her seat.

"Obviously that isn't true, though." David said, absently playing with his knife.

"What makes you say that?" Victoria sat up and focused her attention on David.

"Why start with the minister of antiquities? Why now, a

few weeks before the US president comes to visit? Seems… strange. I mean, why not take out the Russian ambassador any day of any week in any country? Why this minister, in this country, just before all the world leaders descend? It's just not logical." He shrugged.

Victoria looked so taken aback, that Molly intervened with what she hoped was a soothing voice. "Maybe you should get on the case? Get that Pulitzer? You're right here, on the ground, in the thick of it. You should get to the truth.

"You know, you're right. My boss told me to stick to the fracking, but when did a Pulitzer-winning journalist listen when she's told to stay away from a story?"

"Exactly. That's the spirit!" Molly said with a smile.

"So if you hear anything from the embassy, or your contacts, you'll let me know? Off the record, of course." Victoria said.

Molly opened her mouth to answer, but a huge crash from the kitchen made them all jump. David made himself stay seated, but he was poised to jump up if necessary. Maybe the Russian had come back through the kitchen. Maybe…And then a laugh came from one of the servers, and an old man lightly slapped the back of the head of a boy who emerged from the kitchen, red in the face and ducking to avoid the swipe he obviously knew was coming.

All three of them seemed to relax.

"So you were sent here to cover fracking? What are you hoping to find out?" David asked as their food arrived.

"Someone's going to make some big reveal about the relative safety and sustainability of fracking at the energy talks this afternoon. So my boss wants to be on the front line for that because there are planned fracking sites all over our region. Seemed like a good place to get it straight from the horse's mouth.

"What about you? How did you two meet?" Her eyes sparkled as if she was expecting some scandal.

Molly smiled. "We actually met last year, but bumped into each other last night at the party. It was quite unexpected." She reached for David's hand, and he took hers, wondering at the normality of the situation. Molly was basically introducing him as a boyfriend. Equal measures of pleasure and anxiety fought for dominance inside him. As her eyes glowed, the former took control.

He squeezed her hand back. "A happy coincidence."

"That's so romantic," Victoria said, half-whispering in what David could only describe as a wistful tone.

"What about you? Are you married?" he asked to deflect a little of the discomfort that inched down his spine at being the center of attention.

"Boyfriend. But really I'm too busy to commit to anything right now. After all, I'm here, and this is the third trip I've done this month. My job is not conducive to romance, I'm afraid."

Molly tutted. "I can't imagine anything more romantic than traveling the world, reporting like you do. It must be a dream job." She smiled warmly at the other woman.

A tiny sliver of warmth penetrated David's heart. He loved how Molly was trying to make Victoria feel better about her boyfriend situation, when other women—including several he knew personally—might not have been able to help themselves from giving self-satisfied advice.

"It is," Victoria said, "at least…no. It *is* a dream job. What I do…it's everything to me. So I don't mind the lack of relationships, and the lack of sleep." She laughed and speared a piece of chicken with her fork.

The conversation moved to more general things, but kept circling back to the shooting the previous night. He didn't blame them for wanting to talk about it—it was a form of catharsis after all—but he for one would rather not tempt Molly into saying something she shouldn't in front of someone they really didn't know.

"So where did you two meet last year?" Victoria asked.

Uh-oh. Molly crinkled her eyes at him, and he tried to mentally warn her about saying too much.

"I was at an archaeological site last year, and we met for a few minutes only, really. Right?" She looked at David, although it was clear he wasn't supposed to interrupt. "It was a *really* brief encounter. Barely anything, but then I saw him at the cocktail party and…" Molly sighed, a happy look on her face. "The rest is history."

"So what were you at the party for?" Victoria asked.

David forced a laugh. "Is this for an article? Because I'd rather not be news fodder." He smiled broadly to negate the lack of elaboration.

"A man of few words," Molly said patting the top of his hand again.

"Well sometimes those are the best, am I right?" Victoria laughed.

"Sometimes," Molly agreed. "Now what does *your* boyfriend do?"

Victoria's face fell a little. "Urgh. Boring stuff. A policy wonk. We barely see each other."

Molly leaned toward her. "Isn't that nice though? I've often wondered about those kind of relationships. Long distance, maybe. Where you don't get to see each other much, so you spend your time thinking about the other person until you meet again. Isn't that nicer than seeing one another every day? I always thought it might be."

David stared at her. Did she really think that? He guessed she made sense. God knew he'd spent more than fifty percent of his time thinking about Molly in her absence, and was already preparing mentally—or *not* preparing mentally—to be away from her again. Was that what she wanted? Or was she distracting Victoria from making them part of her story? He made a note to ask her about that later.

"I guess so," Victoria said into her drink. She didn't seem convinced.

"When are you heading home?" David asked, trying to get the conversation back on neutral ground.

"In a couple of days." Her face brightened. "The scientist is giving his fracking talk tomorrow, I think, and then I'll report on it from here, and then fly home."

For a while they discussed the food, and Greece, and how they all wished they had a little down time there to vacation a bit. Eventually, a silence fell as they finished the last remaining morsels from their plates. David reached for his wallet, but Victoria held up a hand. "No, it's okay. I've got this. Expense account. I'll just say you're informants. So you know, make sure you are!" She smiled and left a bunch of euro notes on the table. "I better get back. I'm meeting a new cameraman in twenty minutes. I have to break a new one in almost every trip it seems." She smiled, squeezed Molly's shoulder as she passed, and bid them goodbye.

As she left the restaurant, Molly leaned forward and gave him a kiss.

"What was that for?" he asked, before he could stop himself.

She looked bemused. "Because I wanted to. That's okay isn't it?"

He smiled in response, not knowing what the right answer would be. A guy had to keep some stuff back, if only for his own sanity. A "yes" reply would probably infer that they were in a relationship, and he wasn't sure if that was true. Not exactly true, anyway. And a "no" might cause some kind of hiccup in their recent…physical activities, and he wasn't prepared to put a stop to those, regardless of what the long-term situation could be.

"Want to get out of here?" he asked.

She raised one eyebrow. "Sure," she drawled, ripe with meaning.

"I meant for coffee…but if you prefer…"

She laughed, as he'd meant her to do. "Coffee's great too."

Molly reached into her purse and brought out a five-euro note. "She didn't leave enough for the waiter," she said, as she took a few steps toward the bar at the back. She held out her hand as if to shake the waiter's, but slipped him the banknote.

In an instant he remembered.

David was pissed. At himself, and her. As soon as he'd seen

her pass the waiter's tip, he remembered Molly doing the same to Doubrov. *Fuck.* He'd forgotten about that until he saw it again.

After about fifteen minutes of weaving around squares, street corners, and pedestrians, he found a café with chairs and tables in a square across the road.

She seemed normal, but man he wanted to shake her. Instead he pushed her toward some iron tables in the square. "Sit, stay."

He heard her murmur, "I'm not a dog." Before he disappeared into the shop to place his order. All the while the man was making their coffees he kept an eye on Molly across the small street. What was she up to? She kept checking her phone. Goddamnit. This made him mad. He'd been so wrapped up in her that he hadn't even stopped to consider that she was up to her freaking eyeballs in this simply because *she was really up to her freaking eyeballs in this*. He was sure she was up to her neck in something she didn't fully understand.

The Molly he'd met last year was an innocent. A bystander. But clearly that had changed. He just didn't know if it was worth his own peace of mind to stand with her in whatever shit she'd fallen in. Every part of him wanted to protect her, but the voice of his work therapist telling him not to get involved with anything that wasn't sanctioned also echoed. It was a compelling voice. It was on her say-so that he would keep his new job.

He tipped the man behind the bar and took his two caffé freddos out to the table.

"What's this?" she asked.

"Cold cappuccino," he replied sitting down.

"Did you think to ask what I wanted? Maybe I like tea." She definitely sounded pissed off. "So what's wrong? You switched into automaton-David as soon as we left the restaurant, and you dragged me here as if I'm some kind of suspect in something. What happened?"

He couldn't even bring himself to try to talk her down. He just sighed and raised his eyebrow at her. "You slipped Doubrov something. I saw it, and forgot it with all the—" he waved his hand at her "distractions."

"Distractions? You mean me? Is that what I am?" She sat back in her chair and leveled a look at him.

"Nice try, Mol. Enough with your tangents. What did you pass him?"

She paused and took a sip of the coffee and shrugged. "I don't like tea, actually. I love freddos. I just..." She took another sip.

"You just wanted to be contrary, didn't you?" He put his sunglasses on and relaxed a little. He was going to get to the truth, if they sat there all day. "We should have spent more time together in Iraq." Let her try to chat her way out of it, but he'd get his answer.

She leaned forward. "You were working for the bad guys."

"Not to put too fine a point on it, but so were you." He shrugged, but inside, poking at this wound made him nervous. Making light of his nightmare year working for a private security company that turned out to be full of criminals and murderers felt wrong. But easy. Easier than being real anyway.

"That's so unfair. I didn't even know I was working for the bad guys. You, however, did. Wait. Didn't you?" She shoved her sunglasses on her head as if to see his expression better.

He kept a poker face going. That he was good at. "I had an idea. I just didn't know how bad it was until all the shit went down. And what you saw, that wasn't even the half of it.

Concern etched her forehead as she watched him. He wondered if she was genuine or if she was wondering how to play him. Or if he was just too suspicious of everyone. This wasn't how meeting Molly again was supposed to go down. Amazing sex followed by revelations and suspicions.

"What happened after Iraq for you?" she asked, unwrapping a straw and sticking it in her coffee.

"Not nearly as much fun as happened to you, I think," he said. "I saw you on television. A lot." It had been a sweet torture. Seeing her in his room, on the airport TV screens, her voice speaking to him, had been agony. But the positive outcome of seeing her on TV was that it had fooled his body into thinking she was unattainable.

"Well, Harry thought that the more coverage we got, the safer we all were. If anything happened to us, journalists already had us on their radar. Stuff would have been harder to cover up.

Harry—or Henrietta—Molly's boss, and David's friend's wife, had been smart. And lucky. "No one I ever worked with at the company was scared of being found out. Few were scared of anything. That's why I mostly rolled alone." And that was still true.

"So what happened?" she persisted.

"Not much. I had to give evidence at a few committees, none of which made C-SPAN, thankfully. I stopped my short-term relationship with bourbon and severed my ties with MGL Inc. That was the easy part, as most of my bosses had gone to live in federal prison. There were so many charges." He shook his head. "Then a friend hooked me up with Barracks Security and gave me a second chance doing some good. The company's a good one. Not driven by money. They only take jobs for the good guys. It makes a difference.

"What about you? What happened after the cameras stopped rolling?" He was determined to get to her truth one way or another. God she looked good in the sunlight that dappled her face, shining through the trees, playing light tricks over her lips. He wanted to grab her and kiss her right now. And that pissed him off.

"When we got back from Iraq, our team was sequestered while they rounded up all the ringleaders. Then we were questioned. A lot. Debriefed, over and over. They wanted to know everything. We'd been working for tomb raiders for three years." Her voice rose in indignation.

"Tomb raiders?" he suppressed a grin.

"That's what one of the senators called it. I mean, we never found a tomb per se, but they did take our site research and just plundered those areas, stealing everything they found there. It was heartbreaking to find out what they'd been doing."

"I'm sorry," he said. He'd known she was finishing up her studies at the time, and he imagined that discovering the last three years of her life had been nothing short of criminal must have been devastating.

She shrugged. "The State Department debriefed us, and then I basically went on the speech circuit, warning people about the stolen artifacts and the dangers of private archaeology. And how easy it is to proliferate a country's history across borders. And demanding that the government establish some way to monitor private archaeologists. But, actually, when my speech here is done, I'm not entirely sure what I'm doing next. Harry's taking a break from the company"—her eyes lit up—"She's pregnant."

He smiled. "I know. Matt told me a couple of months ago when I ran into him in Florida. Very good news." Matt was one of David's old EOD buddies he'd met up with again in Iraq at the same time he'd met Molly for the first time. "Anytime I get down, I remember what they went through, and figure if they can make it through hell and out the other side, then I can." Shit. That was a little too much information to share with someone he didn't know if he could trust. He decided to cut to the chase. "Okay. Enough about history. Let's talk about last night. What were you trying to slip Doubrov when he got shot?"

She sat up straight. "Dr. Doubrov? I don't know..."

"Sure you do, sweetheart. And whatever it is nearly got you shot." He moved in for the kill. "I've waited a year to see you, and if you die here, because you didn't clue me in on what you're doing, I'm just not sure I could handle it." True, but also, he hoped, a good enough manipulation to make her talk.

Instead she got quiet. Crap, was she going to cry? Her lower lip trembled, and he wondered what black magic he'd used to make her so emotional. He'd better dial it back down.

"David, I..." Her phone bleeped, and she grabbed it off the table like it was alive. She pressed a button. "Hell...what? I can't hear you. Say again? *What?*"

CHAPTER SIX

It was Brandon Peterson at last, but he was breaking up really bad. "Don't say…I can't help…my flight lands in three… Trust…one. Stay away from…"

"I can't hear you. What?" She plugged her finger in her other ear and waited, but there was just silence. She looked at her phone. The phone just showed a photo of the beach near her house. *No!* He had to call again. Who was she supposed to stay away from? Not one word of his fractured message had been comforting. Whatever he'd meant, she figured she'd better just stay mum until he got there. For David's sake. She didn't want to involve him in whatever she'd gotten herself messed up in. She'd just have to wait for Brandon to arrive and dig her out. Which was three hours, or maybe three days. Crap. Well she could maybe hold it together for three hours. If she could distract David. Everything would be better when Brandon got there. He'd always seemed on top of things during her debrief the previous year, someone she could trust.

At least he was a US official, and presumably he knew what was going on. He could take over, and she could concentrate on giving her speech to some very important and influential people from governments all around the world. Butterflies danced in her stomach as she remembered the speech she had to give.

But then there was David. David, who set her body on fire, whose intensity made her heart pump pure emotion through her veins. David, who was killing her by asking for details that she couldn't give him. She couldn't tell him what she'd agreed to do for the State Department, because she'd been told not to. She didn't know if she could totally trust him anyway. Sure, the sex was great, and he seemed caring, but she didn't really know where his head was.

"Damn," she said under her breath, finally putting her phone on the table.

David paused, and then leaned forward, elbows on the table. He opened his mouth to speak, but someone walked by speaking on a cell phone. He waited for them to pass. "I'm not sure how to tell you this, but you are in danger. The Russian government wants to question you about whatever you were slipping into his hand when he was killed. They are telling everyone that the United States is trying to pick them off one-by-one, and the Greek authorities won't protect you from them. I'm waiting for a call from my boss to reassign me, so it could be just you and a KGB officer in a few hours." He shrugged and leaned back.

She did not want to be alone with the Russians. Just the idea made her start breathing faster. A part of her wanted to tell him everything. Leave every part of her open to him as she had done this morning. It might be her only option. She just needed time. Time for Brandon to get there, time to think.

Was it really fair for the State Department to have put her into this position?

David realized that she'd clammed up good and proper about Doubrov, which confirmed that there was more going on than he knew. She was up to her sweet neck in something, and if she didn't tell him about it, he couldn't help her. The only thing he could do was to keep her safe.

David knew that he was going to have to come up with an exit strategy sooner or later. Sooner, since his objective was to get Molly out of Greece immediately after she finished her speech. He basically had just under twenty-four hours to keep her safe and away from prying eyes. He hated himself for wishing Mal were still here to help out.

After they got back to the hotel and unpacked the few belongings they had, David excused himself to get supplies for their stay. He wanted to keep her in the room until five minutes before her speech, hunkered down and out of sight. And he needed some things for that. Food, drink, and more condoms. He planned on enjoying every moment he had left with her, whether he got to the bottom of her involvement or not. He could see in her eyes that she didn't really trust him, and maybe she was right not to. But the truth was that very few people trusted him, and he'd spent the past year trying to prove to the people around him that he could be relied on. He didn't want to leave Molly with the impression he couldn't be counted on. And to do that he had to be counted on.

His whole job with Barracks Security was to protect people. He never asked what their motives were, or what they were hiding from him. So why should he worry about that with Molly? He was beginning to think that maybe she was right not to tell him what was going on. If he didn't know all her secrets, it would make it easier to leave her as she seemed to want. "No tomorrows," she'd said.

It made for a cleaner getaway.

He hoped.

When he got back to the room, music was playing, faint strains penetrating the closed door. He double checked the door number, and inserted his key card. The lights were dim and the music, some kind of lazy jazz, swelled as the door opened.

Molly stood in front of the window. Dusk was falling, and he blinked a couple of times to make sure he was seeing what he was seeing. She had swept her short wavy hair up into some kind of updo, and was wearing a black, sparkling, floor-length dress and what must be high heels. Rimmed with smoky-gray makeup, her light eyes shone.

"I feel a little underdressed," he said softly, so as not to disrupt the mood.

"Then we're even. I was underdressed at the party, where I should have been wearing this." She smiled and twirled.

The skirt of the dress peeled back into small panels of separate material, all the way up to her thighs and beyond, showing her impossibly high, and impossibly sexy sandals. Jesus. If he'd seen her in that at the cocktail party when he was so sure he'd been hallucinating he probably would have passed out.

She came to a halt, and the dress swung around her just a little, teasing with what he knew was under it. He shut the door and locked it, then swung the metal security bar over its hook.

As he got closer, he realized that the top of the dress was not much more than some kind of see-through black chiffon. He swallowed hard. Her breasts were clearly visible through it.

"It comes with special underwear to preserve one's modesty. But I figured that since we weren't going out…" She shrugged.

He tried to speak but couldn't. He had to clear his throat before he could agree. "You are beautiful."

She swung around in a little half circle as if she were embarrassed. "Why, thank you, kind sir."

He smiled. "I brought food."

Her eyes lit up. "What did you bring?"

He mentally winced as he realized how inappropriate the meal was. "Meat wrapped in pita bread."

She closed her eyes and inhaled. "My favorite. Let's eat."

"How hungry are you, exactly?" he asked, putting the bags down on the desk.

She paused. "I can wait."

"Good answer." He shrugged off his jacket and walked over to where she was still standing, in front of the large French window. "I meant it. You really are beautiful." He reached out and cupped her face in his hands, gently stroking down her neck to her collarbone. It was naked, and he suddenly had a vision of himself buying a diamond necklace to adorn it.

The see-through material was soft and silky, and his hands

continued slowly exploring. Her shoulders, down to her breasts, her nipples already straining against the thin material. He rubbed his palms gently over them with open hands. "When you imagined going to the cocktail party, did it ever cross your mind to go like this? To not wear the underwear designed for it? To let the other guests see you like this?"

Her eyes fluttered closed for a second. "No. Well, it crossed my mind, but only as a fantasy. I had no intention of actually doing it."

"Because it's only a turn-on if people think they're seeing something private, more like a wardrobe malfunction than a deliberate flash?" His voice slowed down, and he stroked a different part of her with virtually each word he said.

"Yes. Yes. How did you know?" she moaned, as he nipped at her nipples through her dress.

He raised his head and whispered hot into her ear, "Because I know you. I see what turns you on as easily as I see what turns me on." David slowly walked around her and found the dress's zip. He peeled it down, slowly, so very slowly, kissing her skin as he descended with the fastener. As he reached the small of her back, the dress fully dropped to the floor, leaving Molly naked except for her impossibly high heels.

Unadulterated desire spread through him, heating his very core so much that he wanted to tear off his clothes just to be able to devour her. He pulled off his shirt in one movement, and opened the French doors in the other. A warm breeze flickered across his chest.

Molly turned slowly to look out of the window. They were so high up the people below looked tiny. For sure, no one could see them unless they had binoculars. She inhaled a shuddering breath.

"Do you like being outside?" he asked, taking her hand and urging her closer to the threshold of the door.

She took another shaky breath, and closed her eyes to the view. His hand stroked along her spine, up and down, up and down, so gently, that goosebumps erupted along her arms. When she opened her eyes, they were glassy. "Do you think anyone can see us?"

"Maybe. Would you like them to see me touch you?"

She bit her lip and nodded. His dick was already as hard as he'd ever felt it, but he wanted the moment to be hers. For now. He stood behind her and lightly pinched both her nipples between his fingers. She leaned back into him as he shucked his shoes and pants and continued playing with the tight nubs.

A car's horn echoed through the square they were looking out on, and Molly jumped slightly. David knew that certainly no one in cars could see them, but he was sure that it was probably adding to her fantasy.

He nudged a knee between her legs and urged them apart. Her ass was pressed into his groin as he snaked his hand to her pussy. She was already so wet his own knees nearly buckled with absolute need for her. He used his foot to spread her legs even farther. This time, he jerked her back, so her ass cradled his dick as he spread his hand over her flat stomach, and slowly reached down.

Molly whimpered as his hand floated around her mound, not touching anything other than the heavy fluid that touched the very top of her thighs. His other hand joined in, wrapping his arms around her. He held her open to the air and took pleasure in the gasp as the breeze played against her clitoris. "David" she moaned. "Touch me."

He withdrew his hands and raised her own arms, wrapping her fingers around the side of the door frame. She stood spread-eagled as he ducked under one arm and knelt before her. He felt light-headed with the need to taste her, to have her writhe and come in his mouth. To have her imagine she had an audience.

His tongue darted out straight to her clit. No fluttering or stroking, but a full-fledged assault. His fingers spread her wide as he pressed, nipped, and thoroughly tongued her into submission. Her gasps and moans drove him close to his own climax. But as she crested her own wave, he pushed two fingers into her, allowing her to ride them through her orgasm. She felt like molten lava around him, and he wanted nothing other than to feel his dick inside her.

"Jesus, David. What have you done to me?" she breathed, as he rose and took her in his arms.

"I'm not finished yet, babe. I'm not nearly finished with you." He couldn't wait a second longer. He brought her fully out onto the balcony and bent her over, allowing her to brace herself against the concrete railing. In a second he slid inside her, feeling her whole life pulse around him. She ground back on him.

"Harder." Her voice carried lightly on the breeze, belying her obvious need. He thrust into her hard, and she met every stroke. He couldn't tell where she ended and he began. She felt like a part of him, as if he could feel her arousal as well as he could his own. His desire for her amplified by the second when they were joined together. Electricity thrummed through his lower back, sparking a reaction in his balls. As if she knew, she reached back and squeezed them. Heat fritzed through his spine up to his head as he came inside her, pulsing, throbbing, and flooding her with his naked desire. As he finished, the walls of her pussy gripped him as she came again. Sharper and faster than before.

He brought her upright, so she could rest against his body, and he held her around her waist, and looked out at the city.

"Do you think anyone saw us?" he murmured into her ear.

She giggled and turned to him, hugging him close. "I don't know." She hid her face in his shoulder, and he guessed that now the erotic moment had slipped by, she was a little embarrassed. She was such a contradiction. All roaring blatant sexuality, followed by a slight shyness.

He took her back in, and grabbed a fluffy dressing gown that the hotel had left artfully fanned out on the bed. Wrapping it around her, he kissed her forehead.

"Dammit all to hell," she said.

Alarmed, he stepped back. "What? What's wrong?" he looked around the room to see what could have elicited her comment, but her eyes were on him.

"I thought if I wore high heels you wouldn't be able to kiss me on the forehead anymore, and that you'd have to kiss my lips."

Shame flooded through him. He hadn't even kissed her before taking her out on the balcony. He raised her chin and kissed her gently and slowly on her mouth. Warmth rushed through him like the desert sun. He teased her tongue gently with his. Without the immediacy of sex, it felt more intimate. More like a declaration. It didn't stop him.

CHAPTER SEVEN

They awakened late, very late, the next day. Molly was glad she'd slipped a DO NOT DISTURB sign on the door before they'd finally switched out the lights.

They'd slept, clasped tight in one another's arms, as if warding off the rest of the world. But they slept fitfully, waking every couple of hours, kissing, caressing, and then drifting back off to sleep. It had felt like she was living in a different world than she had a week before. Everything had changed, some of which she loved, and some of which she hated. It was the contradiction that was keeping her restless, and she knew that her tossing and turning had kept waking David too. But this was her big day, and the start of a new…something.

The G20 speech was the last scheduled talk on the tour she'd done, and she had nothing planned after she left Athens. Harry had work lined up for her if she wanted to take it, and last week she'd had every intention of helping out on an excavation in Indonesia, even though that culture wasn't her specialty.

But with everything that had happened, she felt less certain about her future. Less certain about everything. Less certain she'd even survive this week, with the Russians seemingly convinced she'd had something to do with Alexandre's death.

They ate a late brunch, quietly reading the newspaper that had been delivered with the food, and saying little. It was as if they were already prepared to say goodbye. And yet she still didn't really know what they were going to do after she gave her speech.

The newspaper strangely didn't have any articles about the bombing and Alexandre's assassination. She supposed that was good. When they'd turned on the television, the same was true. The G20 meetings had been relegated to third place in the news. A new presidential nominee and a flood in a southern state had taken the top spots.

"This is good, right?" she asked David.

He nodded thoughtfully. He'd made her promise that if the news was heavy on the incidents in Athens, then she'd agree to cancel her speech and leave with him. "Yes, I hope so." A frown furrowed his brow though, and that did nothing to ease the tension in the room, or ricocheting around her mind and body.

Thirty minutes later, she changed into her light blue business suit and silk blouse while David waited at the window again. When she came out of the bathroom she was gratified to see his double take. He'd never seen her in anything so…normal.

"You look amazing. Authoritative. You're going to rock this speech…Then we're breaking for the border, all right?" he said, still looking tense.

She sought to reassure him, even though she was feeling as uncertain as he seemed to be. "I'm all ready to go as soon as I finish. The bellboy will come for my bag and they'll leave it in the lobby for us to grab on the way out." She wondered if she should try to find Victoria to explain that she was leaving. She'd have to look for her downstairs.

He opened the door for her, and she walked through. Grabbing her arm, he stopped her short and planted a knee-melting kiss on her lips. For a second, all thoughts of speaking before a group of government leaders evaporated. She moved close to him and dug her hands into his hair as he deepened the kiss. The smell of his skin was intoxicating. She wanted him so much, and briefly wondered if they would have another chance to make love before they disappeared back to their own worlds. Her heart constricted at the thought, but she pushed the feeling aside. Better to have one perfect day with him than months of uncertainty.

They took the elevator to the lobby, David staying very close to her, every step she took. The comfort that gave her allowed her to concentrate on her speech. She'd emailed it to the teleprompter guy already, so all she had to do was remember to introduce herself.

"You're going to be great, sweetheart," David whispered in her ear, as they entered the auditorium in the conference center of the hotel. Probably about fifty percent of the audience had already taken their seats. She'd been to enough of these events to know where to sit and wait to be introduced. She opened her handbag to grab her index cards, which were now somewhat battered by their frequent use. David squeezed her shoulder and took a seat about ten rows back on the end, presumably so he could make a quick getaway if needed.

She recognized a minister from Egypt and the culture and antiquities minister from Greece as they took seats with their small entourages. The head of the British Museum was chatting to one of the curators from the Louvre. Several prominent archaeologists were present too, and that was what gave her the biggest thrill. Her peers coming to listen to her speak.

The room filled up quickly, and she concentrated on her notes. She'd written a new first card, one that the teleprompter guy hadn't received, so she didn't want to mess it up.

The director of the archaeology museum in Athens took the stand. "As you know, Dr. Solent, our speaker this evening, helped foil a company's plan to loot an archaeological site and sell its artifacts on the black market. And in stopping this outrage, she uncovered years of illegal antiquity trading. She graduated from the University of Pennsylvania with degrees in archaeology and geology. She did her masters at the University of Chicago with a focus on Medieval Europe and her doctorate in archaeology at Oxford University with a focus on Ancient Greek texts." The director paused and smiled. "I'm not at all saying that she is more qualified than me, but you will have to pry this job out of my cold, dead hands, Dr. Solent." Laughter rippled through the auditorium. "Needless to say, she is uniquely qualified to speak to us today. So without further ado, I present Dr. Molly Solent." He turned to her, joining in the applause, and walked from the stage.

She walked up and smiled at the audience. "Before I start, I'd like to pay tribute to Professor Alexandre Doubrov, a beloved fixture of our field's conference circuit, a mine of information, and a willing sharer of his vast experience. He was killed yesterday, here in this hotel, and we have no idea why. Alexandre, you will be missed." She paused for a few seconds before continuing.

"The worst thing about working in our field is the absolute knowledge that there are people who are willing to steal and trade the most valuable parts of our cultures. To rob citizens of the right to their own past and their own history. To rob scholars of the opportunity to study their countries' legacy and to learn from it. It is both an intellectual and a physical crime."

She held her audience rapt in her point of view. No one fidgeted, no one rustled papers, and no one looked at their watches. David felt inexplicably proud of the way she held herself on stage, how she kept their attention, and how she spoke with such passion. He looked around. He felt smug that he was almost certain that he was the only one present who had experienced all of her passion. Jesus. Even thinking about her gave him a semi.

His phone vibrated in his pants, and he got up carefully and made his way to the door so as not to disturb anyone. Once the door was closed behind him, he answered it.

"Church."

"David. How are things going there?" It was Baston, the owner of his company, and his boss.

"About as well as you would imagine," he answered, not wanting to give anything away to the few people lingering in the lobby.

"I hear there's been an arrest warrant issued by the Greek police. For your friend." He said it almost casually, like he was telling them she'd been invited to a clambake.

"I did not know that. How long ago?" His heartbeat kicked up.

"An hour or so. I think the Greeks are under a lot of pressure from the Russians right now. Regardless, Church, this isn't your fight. I've seen the footage, and it looks like she was into something."

No kidding. David replayed the scene in his head. Molly trying to slip Doubrov some kind of note.

"You've seen the footage?" David winced. That meant he would have seen David go for Molly instead of his principal.

"Just come back immediately. I need you in the office tomorrow morning. You're being reassigned. You have no backup there. Mal's already deployed elsewhere. You haven't officially gotten into any trouble yet, but associating with someone wanted for questioning in relation to an assassination, well that might just be pushing the limit. You get me?"

"I get you, sir. I have plans to be at the airport in a matter of hours." He omitted that he was going with Molly, but at least that gave Baston plausible deniability.

"Good. See you in the morning." He hung up.

David looked at his phone. He'd basically agreed to leave Molly. He glanced back at the door to the auditorium and heard people laugh. She must be rocking her speech.

This was the right thing to do. Put her on a plane out of Greece, away from her arrest warrants, and say goodbye. It was the best for her, and the best for him. He still needed to get himself on firmer ground. But right now he had to get her away from the hotel before the police came. Christ, couldn't they have a minute without having to run and hide from someone?

He slipped back into the auditorium, in time to see Victoria enter from the opposite side. They met each other's eyes, nodding acknowledgment. She took a seat at the back, and David took his original seat.

Molly was showing a slide of a woman depicted in a mosaic, as David planned their escape. He'd get the bellboy to pull David's SUV to the back of the hotel. He figured that at least some people would know exactly where Molly was, so time was of the essence. It wasn't like her speech hadn't been on the G20 agenda for months.

Applause startled him out of his plan. Molly stepped away from the podium and nodded, smiling at the crowd. She stepped down from the stage and headed toward him. He jumped up and opened the door for her. "We've got to go now. They've issued a warrant for your arrest.

"What? Why?" she asked trying to keep up with him.

"Don't. Just don't pretend you don't know what this is about, okay? Not with me anyway." He turned away to pick up both their wheeled suitcases from the bellboy, slipping him a twenty-euro note and the car keys before asking him to drive it around the back entrance.

"Come on," he said striding toward the doors that took them down to a kind of loading lobby and out to the back door. He dropped the cases outside the sliding doors and they waited.

"Here," David said, nodding toward the approaching SUV and picking up the bags.

A flare lit under the car, and in front of his eyes, the whole vehicle exploded with a white-hot blaze.

Boom.

He dropped the bags and grabbed Molly to shield her from the heat of the blast, pushing her back through the doors and turning his back to the explosion. Glass and burning material showered down around them, but David's mind was already working at a hundred miles an hour.

It wasn't a firebomb. It was an expertly placed explosive device, designed to totally annihilate anyone sitting inside. The whole vehicle had been destroyed. No chance for the bellboy. Someone definitely wanted them dead.

CHAPTER EIGHT

Sirens sounded, and people came running around the corner into the alleyway. Her ears were still ringing, and the skin on her arms was red where the heat from the blast had hit them.

"We've got to run," David said. "Leave your bag."

"Give me a second." There was no way she could run anywhere in her high heels, not on the cobbled streets of Athens. She ripped open her bag and kicked off her heels, grabbing her sneakers and slipping them on.

David slapped her ass, not once but a few times. What the...? "This is not the time—"

"Your skirt has embers on it." He slapped her a couple more times and rubbed his hands on his jeans. "Come on."

She didn't take the time to look at the state of her skirt, but grabbed the sundress that was on top of her clothes, and took his offered hand.

David took off with her half a step behind. They ran away from the debris, and the people who were shouting and pointing, and headed to the loading dock. Once they'd cleared the hotel block, David slowed, but still ran.

"Smile," he said, as they passed late night shoppers. He grinned at her and she smiled back, wondering what the hell he was thinking.

They continued to run, laughing and smiling until they reached a residential neighborhood. David stopped. "I think we can stop here. Are you okay?"

"I think so. I'm not sure." She was being honest. A poor man had just got blown up, and yet she was glad it wasn't her and David. Which made her feel like an awful person. And someone was obviously trying to kill them.

David grimaced and rolled his shoulders.

"Are you all right?" she asked.

"Sure. A little blast shock, but I'm fine. I've seen worse." He turned to look at a bus stop street map, and she saw his back.

"Jesus. Your shirt is shredded! Let me look"—she pulled up one of the ripped tails of his shirt and saw his back was red raw—"It looks like you have really bad sunburn." She winced at the pain he must be in.

At that second his phone rang. He dug it out of his pocket and answered. "No. We're both okay. They've what?" He nodded a few times. "Thanks, Mal." He paused. "Just fuck off."

He shoved the phone back in his pants and paced in front of the church they'd stopped in front of. "They've closed down the city. No one in and no one out. The police have road blocks on all the roads leaving the city."

"So you don't think we'd make it to the airport?" she asked, wondering what had happened to her life in the past two days.

He remained silent, obviously processing this new information. She didn't press him. She sat on the small wall of the church and took a breath. That poor bellboy. Why would someone bomb their car? Was it because of Brandon's note? Did she set off the chain of reactions that led to that poor man's death?

David stopped pacing and crouched in front of her. She tried to keep her eyes on his face, but her imagination was working overtime. Did the man have family? Did they know yet? "Okay, this is the plan. We're going to take the metro to Piraeus port, where all the tourist boats set sail to the Greek islands. You're going to take out as much cash as you can at an ATM and then you're going to use your credit card to buy one ticket to the farthest island we can find. That way they'll think that you've left the city and we've split up."

She recognized that he was detailing a plan, and she could hear the words, but she couldn't concentrate on what he was saying. The car kept exploding in her mind. *Ka-boom.* And then that second of silence, followed by the clang of falling car parts. Over and over. She tried to visualize what the bellboy looked like, but she couldn't remember if she'd ever seen him.

"We can't go to the airport, and frankly the boats would be easily caught by a police launch, so the best thing we can do is hunker down somewhere anonymous and try to figure out what the hell is going on." He pointed down the road to the metro station, and then looked back at her.

She nodded, because that's what he was waiting for. She was sure it was an excellent plan. He took her hand and led her to the metro station, buying two tickets with some coins.

She was still carrying her sundress, which she understood looked strange, so she folded it up as small as she could and clasped it in one hand as they sat on the train. She played with the buttons of it. What had she done? Had she killed the bellboy?

Wordlessly she slipped her hand in her pocket and passed David the envelopes that Brandon Peterson had given her.

His back hurt like fuck. Like someone had taken a blowtorch to it. *Throb, throb, throb*, in time with the motion of the train. Molly slipped her hand into his, and he took a deep breath of relief that she was still alive, that they had escaped death by virtue of tipping a bellboy to bring the car around.

He looked down at their clasped hand and a coldness trickled down his spine. There was something else in there too. He met her eyes, which looked as though wariness and pain were weighing her down. Hooking his finger under the paper between their hands, he slowly dragged it into his lap.

It was one, no two small envelopes. One had been opened. They had her name on them, small enough to be a florist's card. He opened the flap as she looked away. Inside was a small card.

Stamov extraction.

He was pretty sure Stamov was the Russian finance minister, and he suspected that his "extraction" wasn't referring to a visit to the dentist. He flipped the card over. The other side was blank.

What was a State Department employee doing contacting a foreign minister through a civilian? And why was he leaking what would probably be classified information?

He opened the other note.

Andropov extraction.

He thought Andropov was the Russian prime minister—yeah, that rang a bell.

He gave them back to Molly and took her hand again. They'd talk later. Much later, when no one was listening.

So the Russians were telling everyone that they were under attack from the US. Someone in the US government was warning them that it was true, and now someone was after Molly and David. At least he knew why, now. Someone very definitely didn't want Molly to give that note to someone in the Russian government. And that was either the CIA or…*Fuck*. He couldn't get his head wrapped around it.

Not that he necessarily trusted the CIA to do what was right in any given situation. He'd met too many intelligence officers in Afghanistan who were downright sketchy most of the time. But take down a government by picking people off? Unlikely.

The train terminated at the port city of Piraeus, where Molly took out five hundred euros and then paid for a one-way ticket to Cyprus, which was the farthest island served by the ferries. The ferry would leave just about the time they got back on the metro to return to Athens. It was a good plan, if he said so himself. It would keep anyone from following them and getting them in a pickle. *Another Mal-ism.* It would keep from getting them in a shit-ton of trouble.

They caught the train back to Monastiraki, which was the main tourist area of Athens. Much easier to blend in there. When they emerged from the station, it was dusk, and the partiers had come out to play. Throngs of people ambled in the street, so he adopted their pace and walked with his arm wrapped around Molly's shoulders like so many other couples.

He found a hotel in a graffitied backstreet, just a few doors down from a basement "adult" sex shop. The hotel lobby was clean and well furnished, looking more like a boutique hotel than the façade would have suggested. They checked in using cash and fake names, and eventually were given a key to a room on the third floor. The elevator took an age to come, and when it did they got in silently.

"What did...?" Molly started to say.

He placed his finger on her lips and then claimed them in a kiss. Just for appearances. Just in case there was an elevator security camera. *Yeah right.*

A bolt of longing, need, and relief wrapped itself around his heart as she rose on her sneakered tiptoes and leaned into the kiss. Despite everything that had happened, this degree of need took him by surprise.

The door pinged loudly as it opened, echoing around the small space. Molly jerked away from the kiss, looking mussed and flustered, but there was no one there. No one in the short corridor either. He grabbed her hand, wanting to get a lockable door between them and the world as fast as possible.

As soon as the door swung shut on them, he lifted her up by her hips, finding her mouth again with his, because there were no words for what had happened. She kissed him back with a ferocity that lit a fire inside him.

He wanted to rip her clothes off, but he didn't know how long she could wear the sundress alone, how long they would be there, so instead he put her back on the floor and carefully, with shaking hands, undid the buttons of her blouse.

She batted his hands away and whipped the silky thing off over her head. The beige lace of her bra made her seem naked for a second. He trailed the backs of his hand lightly over her arms. Her skin was warm, alive to his touch. Alive. Thank God they hadn't evaporated into the night air in the car. He shook his head for a second to clear the image of the explosion, but instead his brain took him to his friend Danny, who'd been blown up in Iraq. They'd been dicking around…until they hadn't. Until Danny was gone forever. And they could have been too.

Molly took his face in her hands and he was back with her, yet overwhelmed with the euphoria of being alive. He tried to rein in his impulse to crush her to him, but when she looked in his eyes, she must have seen something. She stepped back and unzipped her charred skirt. In a second she'd wrapped her arms around his neck, dragging him to her mouth.

Proof of life had never felt so good.

"I need you now," she murmured against his lips.

The lady didn't need to ask again. He sat her on the small dresser next to the window and yanked off her panties. He shoved his own pants down and her hand reached for him while she was wriggling to the edge so she could get closer.

She drew him to her, but he took her hand away and put it behind her so she was leaning back. He ran the tip of his dick over her clit, watching as her eyes fluttered closed and her mouth dropped open.

His body blazed with a need to consume her. He pushed

into her in one hard stroke. Heat shot through his balls into the base of his spine. He was going to last no time at all…

He held himself in place, feeling her body pulse around him. "Maybe someone's watching us through the window," he said. "Do you want me to open the curtains a little farther?"

She started for a second and then relaxed, her breathing kicking up as she twitched around his dick. She gazed into his eyes and gave an almost imperceptible nod.

It was all fantasy, the window faced a wall, but he pulled the net curtains open, flicking them across her back as he did. "Take your bra off."

She didn't hesitate, she unfastened it, and allowed it to fall to the floor.

He pulled out of her slowly and grabbed her legs, swiveling her so she was lying across the dresser, giving the wall, and her fantasy, a better view.

He bent over her and dragged a nipple into his mouth. He held it between his teeth and flicked his tongue over its hardness.

His dick strained up, and he was thankful that she was in no position to grab it. He had no idea if he'd be able to hold it together if she did.

Her head fell back, and he wondered for a second if she was imagining someone else watching them. The thought sent waves of arousal through him that took him by surprise.

He gently bit her other nipple and plunged his hand between her legs. Jesus Christ she was so wet. So fucking wet. He dipped his head to her and ran his tongue and fingers over her clit.

Her legs dropped open to give him more access. He'd never been with a woman so open to his touch, so comfortable with her sexuality. It nearly blew his mind that she was his. He knew there was some mental correction to do there, but his mind was consumed with the taste of her. His dick ached to be inside her again. Literally throbbed to feel her hot and wet around him.

He plunged two fingers inside her and curled his fingers behind her clitoris. His whole mouth covered it, stroking it with the flat of his tongue.

Her breath became audible, and then she gasped his name as she contracted around his fingers. He didn't wait for her spasms to recede, he moved her back around so she was sitting at the edge of the dresser and just took her. No tentative pushes, no gentle strokes, just one thrust that blasted through his brain with stars and heat.

God, he needed to be farther inside her. He picked her up and laid her across on the bed, holding her legs open for him. He thrust, hard, his balls slapping against her. She moaned and raised her butt, giving him those all-important millimeters of access.

Everything in him tightened. Molly grabbed her breasts and, with her thumb and forefinger, pinched her nipples, her eyes on his. That was it. While hot heat pulsed from his lower back all the way up his spine to his head as he came. *Fuck, yeah.*

"You're amazing," she said, pulling herself up on her elbows. He felt her deliberately squeeze his dick. He eased out of her, by habit grabbing his dick to keep the condom on. Except…no condom. It hadn't even crossed his mind. Not even once. He'd never had sex without a condom. That was one thing that was beaten into them at bootcamp.

"Molly. I didn't use a condom. Are you...?"

"It's okay, I'm on the pill. And I swear I've been celibate since I met you. You bastard." She shifted on the bed and laid her head on the pillow.

Relief...*didn't* flow through him. What was wrong with him? He climbed on the bed and lay next to her, pulling a sheet over both of them. "Why am I a bastard again? I mean, you're probably right, but why?"

"After I left Iraq, I looked for you everywhere. I don't mean I looked for you online, or tried to find out where you live...I mean, you said you'd come find me, and I trusted that you would. I expected to find you on my doorstep every time I came home. When I wasn't at home, I thought I saw you a hundred times. But it was never you. You ruined my whole year." Her voice dropped to a whisper as her eyes drooped closed. "That's why you're a bastard."

Her breathing changed almost immediately, and she was asleep faster than a cat. He didn't even get the opportunity to apologize, or explain, or revel in the fact that she'd been saving herself for him to show up. That he'd wasted a year. He imagined for a moment what that year could have looked like. Sharing a bed, a home, a life. His last thought was of him and Molly on a sofa, just watching television. So mundane.

So fucking amazing.

CHAPTER NINE

She woke as the light came in through the window they'd left uncovered. She smiled as she remembered the sex last night. He blew her mind. She visualized for a second that someone had been watching him go down on her. Heat pooled between her legs again. What was *wrong* with her?

They were in trouble unless something happened, but all she could think about was David and his talented tongue, dick, and fingers. If she were going to prison, she'd at least have a lot of great memories to pull from while serving time.

David turned over, grabbing her and spooning her from behind. She moved, allowing him to get comfortable, and then settled back against him. His arm was wrapped around her waist, and her whole body was held against his.

He released the tightness around her waist and twisted his arm slightly, just so that it brushed her nipples. They sprang to life almost immediately. Was he even awake? His breathing was deep and steady. He had to still be asleep. He rolled his arm against her nipples again, causing her to bite back a whimper. He said nothing, but gently moved his hand so he could stroke the top of her breast, all the way to her nipple and back again.

She was torn. Should she stay still and let him drive her crazy in his freaking sleep, or wake him up?

He gently touched her again, and she strained for more contact. Her breasts felt flushed, and she was almost tempted to touch them herself. He seemed to love watching that yesterday.

Instead his fingers trailed down her belly, caressing the slight curve of her. He must be asleep. His touch was so lazy, so gentle. So unlike him. She moved a tiny bit, so that if his sleeping self wanted to go further he could. How brazen was she being, anyway?

His fingers slid down the top of her thigh, gently making patterns that were driving her crazy. He shifted against her so that she was almost lying on her stomach, her upper leg now bent to stop her rolling completely on her front. *Please. Touch me.* She could feel her own wetness without even touching herself.

He stroked her ass cheek, over and over until she wanted to scream.

Just when she couldn't take any more, he dipped his fingers, so lightly, first lightly circling her ass, then the side of her thighs, back to her ass, so lightly touching that she wondered if she was imagining it.

But no. He trailed down her leg, and when he brought his fingers up again, they stroked her outer lips, before delving farther in with his return stroke. He hesitated and felt her wetness again. A groan rumbled through his body, but he did nothing except play in the wetness, making her crazy. Then he used three fingers to lubricate her clit. She was so excited she was going to come any fucking moment.

Just when she thought he was going to let her come, his fingers pressed back to her ass, pushing gently for admittance. But just when she thought this was going to take a whole other turn, he went back to her clit. Circling it first with his wet fingers, he then used two fingers to play. He rubbed directly on it first, then slightly to one side, which brought a whole new sensation pulsing through her body, then he just used one finger. Lightly playing over it, until she felt herself rocking against his hand, teetering on the precipice before tumbling over in a wave of pleasure, heat, and wantonness.

As her orgasm subsided, she turned. His eyes were fully open, not even sleepy looking. "You were awake this whole time?" she asked.

"You think I do this kind of thing in my sleep? Not too wise when I spent nearly all my formative years sleeping in dorms with other guys."

She laughed. When he put it like that…

"Well you never know," she said. "You might have got this."

She sprang up, sliding on top of him, straddling his thighs and pressing her still-wet clitoris against his hard dick lying flat against his stomach. He jumped. But not as much as when she slid his whole dick inside her.

She sat up, and raised and lowered herself on him. He clamped his teeth together breathing in tightly. "Jesus."

She slipped a pillow under his head so he could see better, because she wanted him to see her. She wanted to be sure that if he left her, then he would have a lot of memories to torture himself with.

She leaned right back so he could see his dick disappearing inside her. With one hand she braced herself, and with the other she reached behind her and squeezed his balls. He groaned, and pumped faster inside her, gaze firmly at the place they were joined. Just when she thought he was going to come, she sat up and touched the base of his dick as it was thrusting into her.

He gripped her thighs as he came, shuddering into her, eyes closed. She was never going to forget him, that was for sure.

He wrapped his arm around her and brought her head to his chest. His heart was still racing. They lay there for a while—long enough for Molly to wonder what he was thinking about. Long enough to remember what they were running from, what had happened last night.

"My God. Someone tried to kill us last night," she said.

"But they didn't," David said. "And we've definitely done enough here to prove to ourselves that we're still alive, don't you think?"

She could hear a smile in his voice, but his words injected a thread of certainty. This amazing sex was because they were in danger. That's all it was. Their lives were so different, there was no way they could make this work. And despite his best efforts, they were on the run in a foreign country with a few hundred euros to their names. He seemed fine, but she was starting to believe it was because he was calling on his training, and concentrating on the job at hand. She wasn't sure how reliable he'd be if he didn't have a mission on his mind. How…*steady*. She sighed at herself. She shouldn't be thinking about this. She should only be thinking about stopping the death and destruction that had dogged her since she set foot in Athens.

"What are we going to do?" she asked.

"You're going to tell me about that message you were trying to give Doubrov," he said.

She tried to sit up, get off the bed or something, but he held her tight until she relaxed against him. "I was sworn to secrecy," she said.

"Sweetheart. I think that ship has sailed. I need to know what you got into so I can help fix it, okay?" He said, his voice rumbling through his chest.

She raised her head and examined his face for something she could trust. He'd been with the military, so she could trust that part of him, but then he'd gone all rogue with the mercenaries. She knew nothing about the company he was with now, but she guessed she needed to trust him with that part of the nightmare, at least. If he let her down, then shame on him.

She took a deep breath. "After Iraq last year, Henrietta and I were debriefed by people in the State Department. Brandon was a low-level guy who took notes and brought tea and coffee. He was nice, serious…solicitous even. He made sure we knew when the different hearings were and made sure we were where we were supposed to be, when we were supposed to be.

"I heard nothing from him since, until he called me last week. He asked to meet me before I caught my flight to

Athens. He asked me if I would do one thing to help my country. Of course I said yes."

David's mind ran at a hundred miles an hour. Who recruited a civilian to do anything involving the Russian government? His instinct was to beat some sense into the nitwit.

"He gave me the two envelopes and told me to wait for a text to tell me which message to pass to Dr. Doubrov at that cocktail party. And the rest you know. Except I haven't been able to get in contact with him since the professor was shot."

David got up and took the notes from his pants pocket. Brandon Peterson. BP. The fucking pen that had been used as an improvised trigger. BP? But why? Why send someone on an errand and then try to make sure the person she was supposed to deliver a message to was killed? The only reason would be an aborted mission. But then why not just call Molly and tell her to flush the notes?

One thing he knew. He wanted to talk to Peterson. He seemed to be the only guy with the answers.

"What are you thinking?" she asked him, placing a light hand on his shoulder.

He told her about the explosives that he and Mal had found, and the monogrammed empty pen casing that they'd found as part of the device. "I need to speak to Brandon Peterson. And I suspect that he's here in Athens."

She tucked some hair behind her ear, and suddenly all he wanted was to stay and absorb all the tiny movements she made. The scratching of an itch on the side of her nose, the little sniff she made of her coffee before sipping it, pushing her hair off her face. All the little details that made a memory real. That gave it depth. He closed his eyes against the thought that he was collecting memories. Preparing never to see her again.

"What can I do?" she asked, wrapping a sheet around her. It was the first time she'd hidden herself from him. Could she tell he was thinking about being without her? About only having memories to keep him warm?

"You can tell me what he looks like."

"I can do better than that if you give me five minutes." She grabbed the notepad and pen the hotel staff had left by the phone and began to draw.

"You're an artist too?" He was starting to feel decidedly like a one-trick pony next to her.

She looked up from her sketch. "Not even close. But when you're an archaeologist you spend your rookie year sketching what people dig up. I had to go from stick-figures to dimensional perspective in a few short months." She went back to the notepad and smiled as she drew. "Here."

She'd drawn a distinctive looking man. Which made his job easier. He memorized the face. "What does he wear?" he asked.

"I've only seen him a few times, and each time he was in a well-tailored slim-fitting suit." She closed her eyes as if to visualize him. "A battered brown leather briefcase, like an heirloom or something. It doesn't match his dark gray suits and white shirts and dark ties. But he always has it with him."

He lay back on the bed and tried to formulate a plan. Not much of a plan, but he figured if he staked out the embassy, Peterson would show sooner or later.

He swung his legs over the side of the bed and bit back a groan. His back was still sore, and frankly his joints weren't what they used to be. Sometimes he felt like an old man when he got up. All the training and all the explosions during the past fifteen years had taken an unnatural toll on his body. Nothing a run wouldn't fix...which would be fine if he were on vacation.

"Let's see what the news says." He clicked the TV on, pressing the VOLUME button quickly so it wouldn't disturb the quiet ambiance between them in the small room. He looked back at her. Why couldn't they just be simple? A couple who'd met at a grocery store, or through friends, or, fuck, even online. Finding someone like Molly was like finding a unicorn in a boot camp latrine.

"Try CNN," she said. "I was wondering if Victoria might be on. You know how they plug into an affiliate's news feed. Her channel is small, I think, but she's on site, so this might be a much bigger story than fracking."

He found the CNN World station at the end of what seemed like an endless stream of Greek and other European game show channels. His heart sank a little when he realized that the car bomb was in fact obviously the most interesting thing that had happened that day in Europe.

"Turn it up. I can't hear." Molly shuffled forward and sat next to him on the edge of the bed.

He obliged.

"This terror attack has sent uneasy ripples through the international diplomatic community. The G20 meetings are supposed to be a major show of cooperation and solidarity, but this year, in Athens, tensions between Russia and the US seem to be escalating in an out-of-control way. Here's Alex Bernard from the scene of last night's car bomb attack. What do you know, Alex?"

"Well, Kathy, as you say, tensions are high here. We don't know much. The Greek authorities are keeping most of the information to themselves. What I will say is that Russian law enforcement have been invited to participate in these investigations."

"Isn't that unusual, Alex?" the anchor in the US asked.

"Under normal circumstances it would be strange. But with Greece in debt to the European Union, and with Russia offering, unofficially, to cover their debt, the relationship between the two countries has never been closer. Which is causing uneasy undercurrents with the other EU countries represented here. Also, of course, it was the assassination of the Russian minister earlier this week that started this campaign of terror."

Molly grabbed his hand and he stroked his thumb over hers. They kept flashing to footage of the exploded SUV.

"Thank you, Alex," the anchor continued. "And with only just over two weeks to go until the world leaders descend on Athens for the leadership meetings, authorities are looking to wrap up this investigation quickly and bring the terrorists to justice."

David turned the sound down a little. "I'm going to go out for a while, see if I can find Peterson. Will you stay in the hotel and wait for me? I think breakfast is served up on the eighth floor. But you should stay inside."

"Sure, I can do that. Nothing like an excuse to lounge around, I guess."

"Do you need anything?" he asked, as he went into the bathroom.

"Toothbrush and toothpaste. That's all I need, I think. I have my phone, money, and passport in my purse. The only thing I left in my case was my fancy dress and shoes, toiletries and workout gear." She shrugged. "Hopefully I'll get them back at some stage?"

"I'm sure," he lied as he bent to kiss the top of her head. "Take the battery out of your phone, so they can't trace you. I'll be back soon."

CHAPTER TEN

Soon" didn't come quickly. Molly had eaten breakfast, showered, changed into her sundress, washed and dried her panties, dried her hair, read the room's magazines on the balcony, watched some Greek game shows that she made up dialogue for, and napped.

By three p.m., he still wasn't back. She'd gone a little brown from sitting out on the balcony. She'd watched neighborhood people go about their everyday business, which sometimes included taking to the streets with a blanket filled with items they wanted to sell. The small road below her was filled with neighbors chatting and laying out their wares on the sidewalk.

She was starving. Breakfast had been yogurt and almonds with a few cute little pastries that she'd stuffed into a linen napkin and brought up to the room with her. She'd gone up to the restaurant as David had suggested, only to feel totally exposed. She had no idea who, if anyone, was looking for her, but she suddenly realized that she was scared every time someone looked at her face. Not a comfortable feeling. So she'd hauled her breakfast up to the room, locked the door, and put a chair under the handle. She had no idea if that ever worked, but they did it in the movies, so there was that.

She paced the room, wishing for David to come back. She felt safer with him. Even though she still wondered about him. He'd been perfect so far. He'd rescued her, loved her, and kept her safe. What else could a girl want? She felt everything with him. Maybe it was the situation, the fact that she had been thinking about him constantly for nearly a year, but she swore she was falling in love with him. She remembered what she'd said to her friend when she'd first seen David. "Can I keep him?" But it was clear that he still had a long way to go to feel like he could trust himself again. She wondered if it would be best to keep her distance until he could sort out the demons that seemed to haunt him.

She paced the small room, still wanting him to come back. Up and down in front of the bed. Her worst thought, one she'd been hiding in the back of her mind, was that this danger they were in, it was all her fault. She had dragged him into this, without a thought that he might lose his job, or just that she might fuck up his recovery. As this thought bubbled to the surface, she eyed the door, wondering if she should just leave and throw herself on the mercy of the US authorities. Leave David in peace. God knew he deserved it after all he'd been through in the war.

Up and down. Up and down.

* * *

David had been hanging out outside the US embassy in Athens. There was a *lot* of coming and going. He'd identified two other teams who were also staking it out. Russians, of course, and some other team. Probably the Greeks.

He'd done some shopping—a baseball cap for him, and a sunhat and a white lacy shawl for Molly, as well as the toothbrush and toothpaste she'd requested. Hats and jackets—or in this case a shawl—were the best things to be seen in if you thought there might be a chance of someone following you. Easy to whip off and discard, which meant harder to follow.

He was sipping a caffé freddo again and reading a guidebook. Except behind his sunglasses his eyes never left the staff entrance to the embassy. His fellow stake-out teams were watching the people using the public entrance. From his vantage point he could see both, but he guessed they had different priorities. No one who worked there would ever use the public entrance.

He took another sip and pretended to speak to someone on his switched-off phone. As he watched the two entrances, it occurred to him that the hotel room did not have any escape route except the stairs. What began as a slight concern started to worry at him. Maybe they needed an alternative plan. Maybe a bigger hotel in a more built-up area that would allow them to use the proximity of the roofs to make a getaway, like he and Mal had done.

He wondered what Molly was doing. God, just thinking

about her made him hard. He visualized her on top of him, fucking him like she had this morning. His eyes closed for a second; he knew he shouldn't think about sex right now but was completely unable to stop. He thought about the warmness that had filled him when she'd simply held his hand too. He was totally screwed. He knew that now. He just had to persuade her that he was worth taking a chance on.

Just when he'd come out the other end of his drinking and PTSD, she was fucking with his heart. *Brain*, he meant *brain*. Nah, he meant heart. And it was him doing the fucking. He sighed and checked his watch. It was late. He should call it a day and pick up food before heading back.

He finished his coffee and left some euros on the table, picked up his shopping and headed back to the hotel. About halfway there, he felt eyes on him. He stopped to look in a shop window and used the reflection to watch the people who passed him. He turned to go into the store, using it as camouflage while he checked out the street behind him. Nothing. He was becoming paranoid.

The feeling that someone was watching him was strong, but he'd already begun to doubt his instincts. He knew he wasn't one hundred percent mentally cleared, and so did his boss, which is why he'd been on this easy protective detail to start with. He had to keep it together for Molly.

He was tempted to try to get out from the back of the store, but figured that might draw more attention than necessary, so he emerged and continued down the street.

The traffic was bumper to bumper, and within three minutes, he felt equal parts relief and adrenaline when he caught sight of his tail in the side mirrors of the stationary cars. He wasn't losing his mind. Just because he was paranoid, didn't mean they weren't out to blow him up.

Jesus, it was a suit. No idea what nationality. Wait a minute. The mirrors gave him a slightly distorted view of the man, but with the brief glimpses he'd got, the guy could easily be Peterson.

He strode past the street that led to their hotel and continued toward the metro station they'd used the previous day. There was a bridge and a tunnel and a grassy park, all of which gave egress. He turned down an alley that led behind a Coffee Island shop and waited for his new friend to join him. He placed his bags carefully next to a Dumpster and stood with his back against the wall, right at the entrance to the passage. The suit walked a step or two across the mouth of the alley, but David gave him no time to react. He grabbed him by his lapels and head-butted him, then half dragged, half carried him into the shadows.

"Why are you following me?" he asked the man, as he struggled to get up. Under normal circumstances, he would have been sure not to allow him to get up, but he didn't feel entirely on the up and up taking out someone without fully knowing who he was.

"Where is she?" the man said, holding his nose together with both hands.

"Why do you want to know?" So it was about Molly. "Are you Peterson? Are you the reason someone tried to blow us up?"

The man grunt-shouted and stamped his foot in pain. Guess he must have broken his nose. "Fuck," he breathed, shaking his head.

David was fast becoming sure he wasn't a threat. No one prepared to do combat would cry over a hurt nose. He released a breath. "You are Peterson, right?"

"Of course I am. I've been in-country trying to stop this clusterfuck since Molly got here." David didn't entirely believe him. He remembered the BP on the pen.

"Who are you and what were you trying to do by sending a civilian into a shitstorm like this?"

"Are you out of your fucking mind? I need a hospital. You broke my nose." He started staggering to the entrance of the alley.

"Not so fast, dude. If you don't tell me what the fuck is going on, I will leave you here for someone else to find."

"I'm not telling you anything 'dude.' I don't know who the fuck you are, and whoever you are, I doubt you have a sufficient level of clearance. All I've managed to get from your boss is that you're on probation. So forgive me if that doesn't fill me with confidence."

So Baston hadn't fired him for not getting out of Greece, but he obviously wasn't throwing all his faith behind him either.

David had no time for shit. The longer they were in this alleyway the more likely they were to draw attention to themselves. He sighed and as he stepped toward him, he looked away to the street. In his peripheral vision, he saw Peterson look in the same direction. David grabbed his left arm and twisted it up around his back, pressing his face into the wall behind the Dumpster.

"Tell me what I need to know to keep her safe. If I find out you lied to me, you will never be safe. Not here, not when you get back to your cushy apartment in DC. You see this?" He shoved his phone against the wall so Peterson could see it. "There are five people in here, one on speed dial, who can make you disappear forever. You get me? Anywhere in the world. Except for North Korea, I guess. So, you know, you might be safe there. Tell me what you know." He pressed on the back of his head just enough to make him growl in pain.

"Okay, okay. Shit man, don't be a pyscho." David released pressure on him and easily dodged an unpracticed swing from Peterson's fist. It was almost laughable. This desk dude was having a bad day already, and was probably wondering how to explain how he had broken his nose on a surveillance job.

"Really?" David said, raising an eyebrow.

Peterson's shoulders slumped. "I had to…you know."

Yup, David did know. Peterson had to at least try to put up a fight. Quite ballsy for a desk jockey.

"Just tell me what the hell is going on and we can walk away, no harm, no foul." David crossed his arms.

"Maybe for you," Peterson said, touching his fingers to his swollen nose. "I'm going to get you back for that."

"The only way you'll even have an opportunity to do that is if you tell me what. The. Fuck. Is. Going. On." He leveled his gaze at him, trying to impart strongly that his patience was already tissue thin. He took a step toward him, and he raised his hand.

"Okay. Okay. I heard from someone connected to the Russians that there was a big op going down here at the G20. The word was that the US was going to lift the Russian finance minister to get their hands on the Russian banking codes—not for money, but to see which Americans are on their payroll. I'm on the Russia desk, and let me tell you, it's a fucking nightmare keeping diplomatic channels open. No way was I going to stand by and let someone fuck up years of my work with some half-assed mission to get their hands on the Kremlin's banking codes. So I decided to run my own op. Make sure our friendlies in the Russian government were warned."

"Are you a traitor?" David took a step toward him, trying to quell a need to wrap his fingers around the man's throat and squeeze.

"No. It was an unsanctioned mission, no one—and I mean no one, Defense, State, Select Intelligence committee—no one knew anything about it. It was a rogue op, almost guaranteed to thrust us into a war with Russia.

He held his hand up at David's advance. "No. Look. No one at State was picking up any chatter, so they wouldn't believe me, but I knew *something* was happening, and it wasn't going to on my watch. My only way in to warn him was through Molly and her friend Doubrov. I don't have all the fancy contacts that the DOD has. Besides, if it came directly from my office, I'd get fired. Doubrov just had to trust Molly. And all the evidence pointed to him doing so. That's all I know..."

"And no doubt, when they found out you were the one who warned them, your stock would rise in their eyes, right? Maybe they'd request to deal with you specifically, which would raise your stock at State too, right?"

"Why shouldn't I take some credit for stopping an unsanctioned op? I mean..." He trailed off looking thoughtful. Then he shrugged as if he'd thought *what the hell?* "Okay, I believe that the Russians think that Doubrov passed something to Molly, not the other way around. I saw the raw footage. I mean, I told her not to slip him the note, but she did, and if you didn't know it was Molly passing something to him, it could have looked like it was the other way around."

David's blood ran cold. "She didn't pass him the note, we still have both of them." That was the worst news ever. If they thought she'd received some intel from Doubrov, they wouldn't stop until they had their hands on her. "You bastard. All you had to do was call her and tell her to get out. Why didn't you?"

"It was my op. They'd have traced it back to me, and my source—" he looked at his polished shoes.

David put two and two together. "Don't tell me, your source is an unsanctioned girlfriend? Someone you care about?"

"Fuck off. Look, I know it sounds cold, but the op was righteous. If Doubrov hadn't been killed, we would be celebrating a victory right now. If I'd called her afterward and told her to skip town, they would have traced the call in seconds, I would have lost my job, my in at the Russian consulate in DC, and my girlfriend...she'd have lost her job if anyone found out she'd been indiscreet while she was drunk. It wasn't her fault. And she doesn't really know what I do. I just never expected the situation to get so out of hand so quickly."

David grabbed his lapels just one last time and shook him. "You do not involve civilians for this exact reason. You better hope she stays safe, because I will be coming back for you if she doesn't. Understood?"

"Understood."

He released him. "Get the fuck out of here."

CHAPTER ELEVEN

David picked up some more supplies before going back to the hotel. He circled the building once, looking to see if there was any unusual activity. But the receptionist, clearly visible through the lobby window was still playing a point-and-shoot game on his PC. It all felt normal.

He took the elevator up to the room and used his passkey. The door light flashed green, but the door wouldn't open. Suddenly panicked, he dropped his bags and shouldered the door open, hearing a loud crack as he did.

Molly stood just inside the balcony with her mouth open. "I think you just killed the chair." She looked pointedly at the wooden chair that now was in two pieces.

His eyes rested on her in her sundress, braless. He was becoming an expert in her breasts and how they looked in a bra and without. He liked the latter better.

"I'm not sure it's safe to stay another night, anyway," he said putting his bags down. "But first, we'll eat." He put paper-wrapped kebabs on the dresser, where he'd had her the previous night. "No, scrap that. First this." He brought her into his arms and held her for a second, pulling back slightly only to kiss her lips. Her constantly welcoming lips. She opened her mouth to him without hesitation, and she felt like home. *Jesus. Get your mind in the game.*

She pulled away. "I've missed you. But I've missed food more. No offense." She went to the dresser, grabbed a package and sat on the bed, opening it in her lap. He glanced at the briefest flash of the tops of her smooth breasts as she sat, making the top of the sundress gape a bit. He felt like a freaking teenager.

When he turned back to the dresser to grab his food, he caught sight of his smile in the mirror. As much as this couldn't work for them, he was definitely enjoying himself.

"What happened?" she asked.

He took a bite of the kebab, and then wiped his mouth with a thin napkin. "I met your friend. He's in some big trouble, or he will be at least."

She stopped wolfing her food. "What did he say?"

"Nothing much, he just gave me a little background. He's just a desk clerk. He's on the Russian desk now and got some vague intel that no one else would believe, so he just took matters into his own hands. The fall-out we are experiencing right now is why no one lets low-level clerks work in intelligence. They don't know enough to see the big picture. To imagine what could go wrong and weigh the consequences of action versus nonaction.

"Bottom line is that the Russians think that Doubrov

slipped you something, not the other way around. That's why they're after you. His op that was meant to warn Doubrov that this colleague was being targeted ended up getting him killed and started the mother of all international incidents." He paused to let that sink in. "Basically, it's a bad karma blowback of epic proportions. On him, mainly, but also us now. And the US."

She was silent, eyes half closed.

She tried to remember the excitement she'd felt when Brandon had asked her to serve her country. How proud she'd been. And now two people were dead, most likely because of her clumsiness. Two people were dead.

"I should just give myself up. I should turn myself in to the Greek police. Explain. God, I have to explain to the parents of the bellboy." Her chest felt tight, as if there wasn't enough room for her heart to beat in it anymore.

David crouched in front of her. "You can't do that. Brandon's mission wasn't exactly sanctioned, which means you'll have no protection from the US embassy. Which also means that the Russians and the Greeks don't have to play nice with you. Besides which, you didn't kill either Doubrov or the hotel employee, someone else did. We just have to keep you safe until they figure out who did."

She looked into his eyes and saw his sincerity. Nodding acquiescence, she bit her lip to stop herself from crying. He was being so heroic, but she hated that she'd got him involved.

"I'm not going to leave your side. I promise you that. I'll get you through this. It's not your fault." He shook her a little in his arms as if to make sure she understood.

She had no idea what she would have done without him. What if he hadn't been in Athens? That was a fluke in itself. What if he hadn't covered her with his body when the shots started? What if the Russian had taken her off to his embassy in nothing but a towel? Her breath hitched, and she couldn't help a sob that racked through her body.

David stood, moved their food, and sat next to her, pulling her close in his arms. She made a weird noise as she tried to stop the tears. She couldn't. Nothing could. All the stress and anxiety and worry came heaving out of her. Every time she tried to stop she couldn't. She knew her nose was running and she was probably making a mess of his shirt, which made her cry more when she remembered that he had nothing to change into.

"Come on, sweetheart. It'll be okay. We just need to wait until they lift the roadblocks and we'll be out of here. Whether we have to drive, fly, or walk out, it's okay. I'm not leaving you, and soon we'll be stateside again and this will all be a memory."

It was the right thing to say, but it made her cry more. She didn't want her time with him to be just a memory. She hated that she'd got him wrapped up in this, and the fact that the Russians thought that Doubrov had given something to her just filled her with cold dread. She had to keep looking for a way out. She had to keep looking for a way out for David too.

She felt wretched about everything. Except him. David was the only right thing in her life now. He was also the only wrong thing in her life. Everything sucked balls. Sucked giant balls.

Her sobs died down to some rough hiccups, and she blew her nose. She splashed some water on her face, but she still looked like utter shit. "I'm so sorry," she said when she emerged from the bathroom.

He was looking out of the balcony, but not in a "how about this view" way. "Get your things together."

She slumped. Nothing was going to get better. She didn't even care anymore that she absolutely one hundred percent knew that he was about to tell her to run again. She took a deep breath and wrapped up their uneaten kebabs, shoved them in the plastic bag the hotel had left in the closet for dirty linen, stole the small bottles of Korres shampoo and soap, and slipped into her sneakers again. She rolled up her skirt, blouse, and bra, and shoved them all in the bag.

Grabbing her purse, she turned back to him and waited. A siren erupted in the silence, and a car squealed to a halt.

"Yup, they're here for us. We gotta go."

She just shook her head and let him gather his phone and cash. "Come on," he said, grabbing the shopping bags he'd brought in with him. "Stairs."

CHAPTER TWELVE

This was exactly what he'd been worried about earlier. There were a million evade and escape routes in the city, and only one in the hotel. The fucking stairs.

He was slightly concerned that Molly wasn't really reacting to anything after her crying jag. He figured she was due for that, but now she just seemed resigned. At least she was functioning. That was all he needed right now.

He opened the door to the stairwell and peered down. It was clear. "Follow tight," he said. They made it down one floor when the lower door burst open. Two tactical cops came through with their weapons up. Weird for European city cops. But he wasn't waiting to find out what their rules of engagement were. He shoved his bags at Molly, who took them with zero reaction. The stairwell was wide enough that they didn't see him until they rounded a corner.

He suspended himself using the two stairway railings and planted both feet in the chest of the first cop. He propelled himself forward so fast the cop fell back on his partner. They both tumbled down the steps. A gunshot from one of the men blasted into the concrete wall. Shit. Now the other cops would know where they were. His heart rate barely elevated as his SERE training kicked in. Survival, Escape, Resist, and Evade. Right now he was only there for the escaping. "You okay?" he asked Molly, without taking his eyes off the stunned cops.

"Sure," she replied, almost breezily.

"Stay right at my back and be prepared to run, okay?" He leapt over the still-prone guys on the floor, and turned to hold out a hand. She ignored it, mainly, he guessed, because she was carrying all the bags now. Couldn't be a gentleman right now because he definitely needed his hands free.

He contemplated for a second taking a gun from the cop, but given that any crimes involving guns in Europe carried huge sentences, he opted not to.

He peeked through the small round window in the door and saw nothing. He was about to open it when a door burst open a few floors above them. Losers. They took the elevator up. He grabbed Molly by the waist and propelled her through the door. "The kitchen," he said, indicating with a nod. "Go."

They ran together until she dropped back for him to check the kitchen. It was empty except for a guy chopping onions. He looked as if he was about to say something, so David held up his hand and smiled. The well-trained hotel worker smiled back.

They ran for the rear exit. It was clear. He took the bags back and grinned. "Smile sweetheart," he said. If you were looking for a fugitive, your eyes automatically drifted to anyone who looked out of place: shifty, nervous, anxious to be away. So, true to his training, they ambled out of the small passageway and blended immediately with the evening throngs of people commuting home or looking for somewhere to eat.

Dusk had fallen, so it was much easier to merge with the crowd and act like tourists. Out of the corner of his eye, he saw more cops scanning the crowd, so he widened his smile and tried to shrink an inch or two. He was tempted to get her to put on the shawl, and to put on his own baseball cap, but there was no point unless he was sure they'd been identified. May as well save the makeshift disguise until they needed it.

"Where are we going?" Molly asked, as they walked slowly among their fellow pedestrians.

"For the time being, along any street that has the most tourists. Then we have to think about hunkering down for the night. Somewhere no one will find us, and I'm not sure another hotel is an option." He had to call someone. Once they were safe and hidden.

"I know the ideal place. A place I worked at a few years back," she said with an unexpected touch of enthusiasm in her voice. "It's slightly illegal, but I doubt we'll get caught. Now the more I think about it, that seems right up your alley." She was smiling. What a freaking incredible woman. They were basically being hunted by Russian and Greek officials, and she was making a joke.

"Not so much anymore, sweetheart, but bending rules I'm okay with." He cast a thought at Mal, who would have virtually got a hard-on at the thought of being able to do something totally illegal. "I'm in your hands. Lead the way." He wondered what she had in mind, but didn't see the benefit of questioning her about it when there were hundreds of people around.

She led him through the streets of Monastiraki, gradually away from the crowd, past Hadrian's library, and up into what looked like a residential neighborhood. The streets were so small and windy that they would be able to spot someone coming easily. The occasional dog barked as they walked past its home, constantly moving upward, leaving the humidity of the streets below, feeling the lightest breeze as the air got a little cooler.

Finally a street gave way to a dirt path, with a fence on one side and a bare hill on the other.

"We are on the trail to the Parthenon. The other side of the fence is the agora. The marketplace of ancient Athens. It's all mostly ruins now. But if you can get me over the fence, I can take you to our room for the night," she whispered.

That he could do. "Stay here, let me do a little recon." He went searching for the lowest, or least well-maintained part of the fence. Really it wasn't a great security feature, more a vague discouragement of entering after hours, he suspected, when he found a brick post that was pretty easy to climb over.

He easily boosted her up, so she could jump down on the other side, and then followed by using the post as a fulcrum to swing his legs over the fence. Easy.

"This way. Be careful of the tortoises, there are a lot of them here." She took his hand and led him into the darkness. Through undergrowth, across stone floors and small wooden bridges, until he saw the very top of a huge temple lit with floodlights looming ahead of them.

Really?

She ran up some shallow steps to the base of the temple. It was in much better shape than the other temples he'd seen in Athens. "It's the temple of Hephaestus," she breathed, sounding as if she was in awe. "Take your shoes off."

He complied, watching her slip off her own sneakers. She almost danced up the broad stone steps of the temple and disappeared inside.

Molly couldn't believe she was breaking the rules like this. It's true, she had a pass—probably somewhere in the suitcase she'd left at the hotel—that allowed her into the archaeological sites, where tourists couldn't go. Now with the authorities on her tail, she wasn't entirely sure her pass would make much difference anymore.

This was the perfect place for them to stay, though. It was in a gated compound, and she was pretty sure no one would think to look for them there. The lights at the base of the temple that lit its roof for the tourists to see at a distance, let just enough light in to illuminate the interior, just enough that they could see what they were doing.

There was nothing inside, just a sandy floor and a few blocks of stone. "I think we should be safe here," she said, sitting on the ground, leaning up against one of the inner walls and opening the bag she'd been carrying with the kebabs he'd bought earlier. "I'm starving."

David walked around the room, looking out. Although probably in the daylight you could see through the temple, at night you couldn't. As long as they slept toward the sides, they would never be seen. "I would never have thought to come here," he said, sitting next to her.

"Let's hope no one else does either." She handed him his food, and silence fell as they ate. As the kebabs hit her stomach she felt calmer and more settled. She took a breath. And another. They were safe here. And she felt at home here. The last time she'd been inside this temple was when she was at college. But it felt familiar, and familiar was good when everything else that was happening to her was so alien.

They finished their meal in complete silence, except for the ever-present noise of the Athenian traffic. Once the last morsels had been consumed, she asked the question that had been bothering her since their car blew up.

"Are you going to get in trouble for being with me?" she asked. "I mean, with the car bomb and the killing of Dr. Doubrov?"

He paused before answering. "Honestly I don't know. My boss ordered me back to the airport, but that was before they locked down Athens. So right now, my future at the company could go either way. I'm not worried about it though."

She thought that might be a lie, judging by his strained voice. This was the last thing she wanted to happen. He'd just gotten his world back together, and she was the one responsible for knocking it out of whack again. She wondered how she could fix it for him. Given that he was already inextricably linked to her—after all it was his car that was blown up—she wasn't sure how best to do it.

She stood to gather their detritus and crept outside to deposit the plastic bag in one of the trash cans in the agora.

She considered leaving. Walking away, finding the police. She hesitated, looking toward the entranceway, which always had night guards. Then she looked back at the temple to see David standing, watching her, leaning against one of the pillars. "Don't." His voice floated to her on the light breeze.

At the thought of him watching her, her nipples tightened, shooting a small flame of need through her. Her libido was driving her nuts. She never knew she could be so turned on all the time. It was his fault. She looked up at him, and he held out his hand to her in the dark.

She slowly took the steps again, and as she approached him, she took his hand. He bent her arm so that it rested against his chest. "Don't even think about it," he said.

He backed up to allow her back into the temple. She didn't want to lie, or make a promise she wasn't entirely sure she could keep. She was about to change the subject when a light beam hit her. She tried to step out of it, but he stopped her.

"I can see through your dress," he sounded amused. "Your nipples are poking through the material, they're making me want to put my mouth on them. Maybe bite them until you're just this side of the pleasure-pain line. Come here. I want to taste you."

She was hypnotized by his voice. And really excited. All she had on was the sundress and a tiny wisp of material for panties. That fact alone excited her. She moved toward him, as if pulled by an invisible length of string.

Very deliberately he undid the top button of the sundress, showing the very tops of her breasts. Then the next button. And the next. The top of the dress came apart easily, showing her to him. He reached for her, but stopped himself. She almost whimpered.

"I want to watch you. Can I watch you?" he asked in a low voice.

She nodded, feeling like a pool of liquid, just shimmering on the surface, and having no solid mass.

He took off his T-shirt. She'd forgotten how magnificent he was. Broad shoulders, broad chest, and a complete six-pack. Obviously she'd seen him before, several times in the past day or two, but this time she watched him too. How his muscles moved under his skin as he moved.

"Take off your dress," he said simply.

She unbuttoned the entire front of her dress and slowly peeled it off, shucking it from one shoulder, then the other. His eyes never left her. He watched the expression on her face, her shoulders as the dress fell from them, and then her whole body as she stood before him. Never had anyone watched her so intently. Never had she felt so turned on.

"Take off your panties," he growled.

She was so wet for him, that all she wanted to do was to put her hands between her legs for some sweet relief. But instead, she turned away from him, looked over her shoulder to make sure he was still looking, and bent at the waist to remove her panties. She slowly dragged them down her legs until she was resting her hands on the floor. She picked up one foot to take them off, and then placed it down much farther away from her other leg. If he was going to watch her, she wanted him to see everything.

"Turn around."

She turned to face him, totally naked, totally turned on. "Take off your pants. It's only fair." She smiled at him with her best, most innocent smile.

He took off his pants, and as she'd thought, he was commando. His dick sprang free, and her mouth watered at the sight of him. She suddenly had a reality check. She was in an ancient temple, on the run from police—or worse—and the magnificent man in front of her had just dropped his pants. David, who she'd dreamed about for nearly a year. David, who was making her mouth water at the thought of having his dick in her mouth. She was a different person. She didn't care.

"Play with your nipple for me. I want to see how hard you can make it." He leaned against the wall, his hand almost absently stroking his stomach.

She brought one hand up to her breast, but he stopped her before she could.

"Lick your fingers first."

She couldn't help but smile. He was a dream come true. She stepped closer to him, so they were only a few feet apart. She licked her fingers, and then inserted them into her mouth and sucked at them. She heard his breathing change. Victory. Instead of stroking her breasts first, she went straight for her nipple, running her slick fingers around it, and then pinching it until she could actually feel the wetness between her legs. She closed her eyes and moaned.

"Is this how you pleasure yourself when you're alone?" he asked in a hoarse voice.

Her eyes opened. Slowly she shook her head, her hand dropping to her side.

"Show me. Pretend I'm looking in from the house next door. Pretend I was getting ready for bed, and I just happened to glance up to see you. What would you be doing?"

She looked around and perched on one of the large stones. "I'd be doing this," she whispered. She took both breasts in her hands and stroked them with all her fingers splayed. Her fingers came together at the point of her nipples and she pulled them both lightly, pinching them until they throbbed. When she let go of them, they were totally erect, and David's eyes never left them.

Then she moved her legs apart, lying back along the stone. Her hands then trailed down from her breasts, over her stomach, to her thighs. Her fingers danced on her thighs, stroking higher and higher until they grazed the small amount of hair she had there. She could almost feel the heat from her body. Goosebumps erupted as a breeze threaded through the temple. Her skin tightened everywhere, enhancing her arousal.

She opened her eyes. He had come closer. He was just a couple of feet from her, stroking his dick as he watched her. She took a breath and watched for a second. She didn't think she had seen anything more beautiful in her life.

"What? Don't you think that this is what I'd be doing if I'd caught sight of you doing this in the next-door house? I can guarantee that I'd be doing this. I'd try to prolong it as long as possible, so I can see you touch your pussy. Are you going to? I want to see you show me how wet you are right now."

Heat shook through her as she widened her already open legs. Then she used her fingers to open herself to him, knowing there was no way he wouldn't be able to see how wet she was, even in this light.

He took a shuddering breath as he watched her. "I want to see you come. Make yourself come for me, baby."

Her heart jumped and a fire lit inside her. She pulled herself more firmly onto the stone and used both hands on herself. One hand stroked her clitoris, slowly to start, and then faster. Spikes of white heat flashed around her body as her muscles melted against the stone. She pushed two fingers up inside her as she continued to stroke, letting him watch her thrust her fingers in and out. In and out. In seconds she felt herself climb that wave, cresting until her orgasm racked through her body.

Before she'd even stopped shuddering, he was on his knees in front of her, his whole mouth around her, sucking, and tonguing her into another wave. His teeth grazed her already sensitive clitoris as his tongue pushed into her. The overwhelming sensation pushed her into another climax, sharper and shorter this time. She gasped for air, but he gave her no time to relax. He pulled her onto her feet and bent her over the rock. He slid into her immediately, groaning as he filled her.

"Yes," she panted. "Yes, more." She wanted him to lose control, she wanted to feel that power. Her breasts grazed the cool stone as he fucked her. Thrusting into her hard and fast. She tried to use her muscles to grip him, but he was too strong. Too firm in his movements.

His breathing ratcheted up a notch. "You're unbelievab—" he started to say. He gasped out her name as he came, pushing as far into her as he could get.

Molly pushed herself up from the stone, and stretched her

back, arching it and then flattening it again, aware that as she did it she was providing extra friction on his dick. He groaned. "You're some kind of sorceress. I've never met anyone like you." His hands stilled her, and she eased around, allowing him to withdraw.

His eyes were intense, and she wanted to say something funny to relieve the tension, but instead he dipped his head to kiss her. He tasted of sweat and of her. He pulled her to him and kissed her hard, his tongue demanding and controlling, sending shivers through her body. She moaned against his mouth and pressed herself against him. He pulled her into a hug, and nuzzled her neck.

This was the real deal, she was sure of it. And she wasn't going to let him go.

But she also wasn't going to let him be blamed for anything she'd gotten herself into.

CHAPTER THIRTEEN

Come here," he said lazily, watching her look for her clothes in the dim light. He had redressed, well his pants at least, and she was looking adorably perplexed.

"I was wearing underwear, wasn't I?" she asked, eyes still on the ground.

"They were very pretty. Now come here."

She stopped looking and shucked on her sundress, unfortunately. She still looked like heaven to him.

Molly came over and made as if to sit next to him, but he pulled her onto his lap. It was like his rational mind had been totally clouded by her presence. He should be thinking about trekking out of Athens on foot, by night. Every moment he was here with her, he lost time they needed for their escape. But this temple and Molly had cast a spell so deep that he couldn't bring himself to move. Not when she was so close. Not when she was nestled so perfectly in his arms. In a temple.

"We haven't offended anyone by…I don't know…" he started.

"Desecrating the temple?" she asked, with a smile in her voice.

"Yes. I didn't think about it until now." He said. He had enough black marks in his book, he didn't want to add eternal hellfire. Although, no shit, it had been totally worth it.

"No. There are so few worshippers of the ancient gods now. They do exist, but not in vast numbers. Besides which, Hephaestus was the husband of Aphrodite, so I suspect he wouldn't be too shocked."

He loved that she talked about the gods as if they were real, but he guessed it was her work. Why wouldn't it be real to her?

"I'm sure if anyone knew I'd been sitting on that rock, they'd bar me from the country, but I totally justified it in my head because I was naked. No buttons, zippers, or anything else that could damage or scratch it." She paused. "Yeah, I'm not sure they would care about that. I'd still be banned."

He smiled in the darkness. "Totally worth it though, right?"

"Totally."

There was silence as he stroked her back, her skin like silk beneath his hand. "Do you believe in the ancient Greek gods?" he asked.

He felt her shrug under his arm. "Who am I to dismiss a religion that hundreds of thousands of people bought into? I've seen evidence of so many different religions all over the world, and they're not that different. Just people finding meaning in nature, creating rules for themselves that benefit society. They believed in their gods so strongly that they spent generations creating temples to worship them. The temple we visited...God, was it yesterday? The day before? It feels like a week ago. The temple to Olympian Zeus? Took six hundred years to build. That's got to indicate a fairly firm belief system. I respect all religions."

"So if I told you I was a Jedi?"

"I would tell you that all the empirical evidence points to it being a solid belief system." He felt her shake with laughter against him. "But would I have to convert in order to marry you?"

He wanted to laugh, but he stayed silent. Make her squirm. "Um, yeah, err, about that."

She pulled herself up. "Oh God, I was joking. It was a joke. I was just…oh God." She buried her face in her hands.

He let her off, and laughed.

"Were you messing with me?" she squealed, hitting his stomach with her tiny fists. He grabbed them and pulled her back to him.

"Maybe." He said, enjoying the feeling of normality.

"You're awful." She wriggled against him, as if she were trying to find the most comfortable spot.

"Yes I am." He leaned back and tried to relax. But all he could think about was the time they were wasting there. Time they should have been fleeing the city. The truth was, he didn't see an easy way out of this mess. He always had a plan. Always. The military had drilled into him all the possible responses to any situation he could find himself in. And his SERE training would have served him well in this urban setting. Being able to navigate based on the direction TV satellite dishes were pointing, moving in concentric circles, avoiding straight streets, knowing the obvious place to go to for a fast extraction.

But none of his training had accounted for him being a private citizen, being caught up in Molly's blowback espionage, and being hunted by virtually every security force in the city. Even possibly the US government, given he just busted the nose of a diplomat.

But even though every thinking brain cell was yelling at him to leave, every breathing cell of his body was telling him to stay right here, with this woman in his arms. It was a fight that kept him awake, even when he felt Molly drift off.

A boom echoed across the city, and the last remnants of the sound rolled into the temple, bringing David to his senses. He woke Molly up and shifted her to the ground so he could get up.

"What—" She rubbed her eyes. "How long was I asleep?"

"Not more than an hour. Did you hear that?" He tried to see the city from their vantage point in the temple, but couldn't. "That was an explosion. Not fireworks or anything." He looked out from between the pillars but could see nothing. "Where can I go to get a better view of the city?"

"Basically the highest point at this end of Athens is where we came from—the Acropolis.

"We've got to go. That sounded big. Like level-a-building big." Or worse. He motioned to the way they had entered.

"Shouldn't we stay here? This has got to be the safest place, don't you think?" she said, looking around the interior as if he'd asked her to abandon her home.

"Physically maybe," he conceded. "But also we have no alibi for...whatever just happened. And we're already wanted by...well, probably everyone by now. The police, the Russians, the US embassy, FBI..." Not to mention his boss. He wondered if he even had a boss now. He was totally off the books here, and it didn't feel good to him. Mal would be totally in his element here, but David, after the last year, was not.

"That never occurred to me. Maybe we should have stayed in a hotel." She bit her lip as he hurried her out.

"I don't think so," he said remembering the fully armored and weaponized police who had stormed the hotel. "This was the best option out of the two." But he really wasn't that sure anymore if he was making any right decisions for any of the right reasons. What kind of operative let a civilian decide where they would stay the night?

He led them back the way they'd come a couple of short hours earlier, back across the agora and over the brick pillar. Then he followed the path up the Acropolis. The gates to the Parthenon—the famous temple everyone associated with Greece—were locked. Nothing he couldn't scale if he wanted too, but opposite the gate was an unguarded hill. He started to climb.

"Good idea. The Areopagus," Molly said.

He turned back to take her hand. "The what?"

"This is where Saint Paul preached to the ancient Greeks, started their conversion to Christianity. You can also see a whole chunk of the city from there."

Even before they got close to the top he could see a huge plume of smoke pushing into the night sky. An orange glow told him that whatever had blown was still on fire. He could see the Temple of Olympian Zeus from where they were, and he was able to figure out where the explosion had been. As they got higher, faint sirens floated on the air. Constant and worrying.

"Where is that?" Molly asked.

"It looks to be in the vicinity of the embassies, close to the hotel we were in." He was wondering how many people were likely to have been hurt. If it was an embassy, hopefully none, since it was nighttime. If it was the hotel, or any of the other hotels that were packed with G20 attendees, the casualty rate would be catastrophic.

"Listen, do you mind if I…" Molly began.

David couldn't take his eyes off the scene laid out in front of him. In terms of national embarrassment, this took the cake. Having such huge security issues a few weeks before the presidents and prime ministers arrived was the worst thing a struggling country could experience, not to mention the first time in G20 history that there'd been such threats.

"Mind if you what?" he asked, still wondering what sort of device it had been and what kind of carnage it had wrought.

"I need to pee," she said anxiously.

"It's okay, I won't look." Really, he'd seen every inch of this woman, he couldn't imagine why she would be worried about peeing.

"Okay, thank you. I won't be a minute," she said.

In the silence came an epiphany. He was spectating up here. This wasn't who he was. He needed to act. To do something positive. How had Molly distracted him? Made him run and hide? He had to figure out how to keep her away from harm, but until he took the fight to the Russians, he would be sitting atop this hill forever. Well, metaphorically anyway.

Molly had to know someone in Athens, or even Greece, who could pick her up, shove her in the trunk, and get through the roadblocks and out to the countryside somewhere. When she was safe, he and Brandon Peterson needed to talk. Screw his Russian girlfriend. This was beyond that. Peterson needed to come clean, so the blame for these explosions, and the assassination wouldn't land at the USA's feet. Because a new world war, or even just a cold war with the constant threat of nuclear action would taint this whole generation.

This was bigger than him, bigger than Molly even, and dammit, he was going full-steam to the source. He half wished Mal were there. The annoying bastard would be useful right about now. Scared of nothing, and caring about nothing is the ideal state of mind for a soldier, something he suspected Mal knew only too well, if the rumors about him were true. That was the main difference between them. David had been trained to care about his country and his brothers in arms. Mal was mission-focused. Nothing got in the way of the mission. Which was an attitude he could have used right about then.

As soon as Molly got back, he'd make her figure out who she could call to keep her safe while he waded back into the thick of it. Back to his comfort zone. No wonder he'd felt off his game, running from hiding place to hiding place. But he hadn't really had a choice with Molly with him. He didn't fancy her chances with the SVR, that was for sure.

Where was she? She must have needed to pee really badly. And then his thoughts sped up and skidded to a halt when he remembered her face as she took the remnants of their meal to the trash can. He'd been almost certain that she'd been considering doing a runner. Surely she couldn't be that crazy? A slow dawn of reality hit him. She didn't trust him to keep her safe. To give good advice. He couldn't really blame her. He'd broken his promise to her last year, and all he seemed to have done this year was to keep leading her into trouble. The bad guys had turned up everywhere they'd escaped to. She was right. She was dead right. He was useless. Even his company-mandated therapist had told him that he shouldn't trust his instincts until he'd fully recovered. And that's all he'd been doing—using his instinct. His shoulders slumped as he turned, hoping against hope that he was wrong. That she trusted him, that she'd stay with him.

He watched the path she had taken, his heart racing, almost making him light-headed. Come on, Molly, he urged. Please trust that I can keep you safe. Please don't leave. He paused, the weight of his past rolling in waves through his body. He took a breath and tried to shake it off. He was still in the middle of a mission, and he couldn't break down now. He clenched his fists. He didn't care what she thought. He would save her. And then he would have to let her go.

He tried to shake off the lingering doubt he had in his own abilities as he ran back the way they'd come, making controlled slips down the scree on the hill. "Molly," he hissed. He got to the base of the hill, opposite the gates to the Parthenon, and found no one. The path went two ways, broad and flat, and easy for her to run down in sneakers. He took a fifty-fifty chance and went back the way they'd come.

After about five minutes of running, he knew he'd chosen the wrong path.

Maybe the universe was telling him something.

CHAPTER FOURTEEN

Molly had figured he'd choose the path they'd been on before, so she'd chosen the other one. It had been a longer way down, but also more familiar to her. They'd been able to drive up that path with their equipment on a dig a few years past.

She was proud of herself. She'd done something to save David from getting in trouble and losing everything again. She didn't want him to have to worry about her.

Her plan was to make her way slowly to the US embassy by the time it opened, and to sit in the visa waiting area until someone noticed her. It was the best way not to be arrested by the Greeks or the Russians, but to be on sovereign American soil, and hopefully safe. It would also buy David some time to disappear. She figured that with all the sirens at the recent blast site, the number of police out looking for her might be halved or better.

She wandered Monastiraki as the moonlight faded and the

slow rise of the sun started to brighten the sky. Shopkeepers were already sweeping the areas in front of their shops, slopping water over the sidewalks to get rid of take-out food remnants that partiers had dropped on the ground. If she wasn't so scared about what might happen to her in the next day or so, she could enjoy this time of day. The temperature was much cooler, and the air drier and fresher.

She pushed on through the back streets toward the National Archaeological Museum, a good mile or so away from the sirens and David. She'd stayed near there in a bed and breakfast when she had been studying at the American Archaeological School. She was familiar with the streets and rhythm of the day there. Also, her favorite coffee shop would be opening soon.

She hoped he would forgive her for leaving, but it was a matter of life or death for her that he not be involved anymore. It wasn't until he'd made fun of her when she mentioned marriage, that she realized he'd never made fun of her before...never really cracked a joke even. Until then. And she'd understood how hard he'd been working at keeping focused. He was great at his job—and in some ways she could see that it had been his salvation—and she wasn't going to allow him to lose it over her.

People started to populate the streets, and storefronts started to open, including her favorite coffee hangout. It wasn't really a hangout in the normal sense, it was a place with no chairs, just stand-up tables and a bar where people ordered their strong coffee and a pastry and watched a tiny TV screen in the corner as they drank and ate. Starbucks it was not. Most people stayed for no more than five minutes unless they were chatting to someone.

She slipped in an asked for an espresso and an egg custard pastry. The barista wasn't the same one who'd been there a few summers ago, but then Molly didn't really feel like catching up right now. She took her breakfast to one of the tables and sipped the hot brew. The news was playing on the television, and as she ate, she watched the footage of the explosion.

It had been at the Russian embassy. Her heart sank. She couldn't imagine anything worse, although thankfully it seemed no one was in the building at the time, except a security guard. She wondered if they were going to blame it on America, as they had before.

She took a bite of her still warm pastry and chewed slowly. Vanilla cream flooded her mouth with memories of better times. And then she choked. She couldn't imagine anything worse than the embassy being bombed? She could now. She inhaled and choked on a tiny piece of flaky pastry as her face flashed up on the TV screen. She didn't understand much—her modern Greek language was really rusty, but she didn't really have to. David's photo flashed up beside hers, and an icy cold dread washed over her. It wasn't just America that was being blamed, it was David and her specifically. And she'd left David without him knowing. What were the odds that he'd find himself somewhere with a TV? Shit. What had she done? She cleared her throat to try to get the remaining dry crumbs out of her throat, and noticed the barista was on the phone. He was ignoring four or five customers. How long had he been on the phone? Could he be…?

He looked at her, then averted his eyes quickly. Sirens sounded close by. Adrenaline rushed through her as she dropped her pastry and ran. Ran away from the sound of the sirens, and toward a residential area. Suddenly a silent police car pulled out of a side street with only its blue light flashing.

Crap. She dodged down an alley and booked it to the next intersection, straight across that one-way street and down another alley running diagonally. She heard squealing brakes, but she didn't look around. The roads were getting busier now, and it became harder to run past the other pedestrians without banging into them and creating more of a spectacle.

She tried to walk at the same cadence as the fastest walkers, trying to blend in, as David had showed her. She grabbed the light shawl out of her bag and draped it over her shoulders. At least if anyone was looking for a woman in a yellow sundress, they wouldn't see enough of the top half to recognize the color.

Two police cars swung around a corner and started to sweep either side of the road, driving slowly, looking at everyone's faces. Shit. Shit. Shit.

A short alleyway loomed ahead, and she took it slowly, not looking around as she so desperately wanted too. *Look straight ahead. Look straight ahead.*

As she turned the corner onto a new street, she dared look back down the alley. Two police officers were following her on foot, and when they saw her face, they started running.

How long could she be Greece's most wanted? Where was she supposed to run to? She took off, thankful that she was wearing sneakers and not flip-flops. Sirens came from the right, so she veered left. Suddenly an SUV with tinted windows screeched to a halt in front of her. Her heart sank. Okay, she couldn't run anymore.

The driver wound down his window. Holy crap. A familiar face at last. A friendly familiar face. "What…?" Molly said.

"Get in. I'm just glad I found you."

Molly's heart pounded with relief. "Sure. I'm so happy to see you."

"Me too. You have no idea. Get in the back so you can hide."

Molly looked around for police, who seemed to be in the next street along, and opened the door. The Russian was in there with his gun pointed at her face.

"Get in, Ms. Solent, and you might live a short while." All she could see was the shiny gray gun. She took one step backward and the driver door opened.

Her spine seemed to fold in on itself, as she registered a pinprick. Through her blurry focus she saw hands pushing her uncompliant legs into the car.

Shi…

He was absolutely going to kill her when he found her. David paced the streets, knowing full well that it would take a miracle to find her in this maze of a city. The heat swarmed the streets like thermals in the morning sun, deliberately finding him and making him sweat. Not that Molly's disappearance couldn't make him sweat enough anyway. Damn her. What was she planning to do? Turn herself in to the Russians? The Greek police, who were keen to appease the Russian government?

The US embassy? David wasn't entirely sure that they wouldn't throw her under the bus to avoid a huge diplomatic catastrophe. No, he corrected himself. It was more than just diplomatic now. He suspected that this kind of incident at a G20 meeting, could do nothing less than take them to war if the Russians found any evidence of foul play.

He really only had one play left. And that was far from a sure thing. Damn it all to hell. Damn Molly all to hell. What had she been thinking?

He slipped the battery back into his phone and called the number on Brandon Peterson's card. It was a long shot, since it must be nearly eleven p.m. in DC. The call was picked up immediately.

"Mr. Peterson's office," a soft voice said.

"Can you patch me through to him please? It's important."

"Who is this please?" the voice asked with a hint of stress showing.

"I'm in Athens, and I think we both know that he is not sleeping. He has a broken nose, and I suspect he's been waiting for my call." That was a total shot in the dark too. But he couldn't imagine for a moment that this wasn't already a huge topic of conversation in the State Department.

There was a couple of seconds of silence. "I'll see if I can connect you."

David looked at his phone for a second and said a mental goodbye. Did they have the equipment on hand like that to trace his phone? The clock on the display said he'd been waiting twenty seconds. Thirty. How long did it take to dial a phone and transfer his call?

As he waited, he paused by a bus stop slowly crowding with people.

"Who is this?" Peterson's voice pierced the quiet in the street.

"How's the nose?"

"You better come in, Church. And bring the girl with you." He definitely sounded as if he was trying to impress a room full of people.

"That's the thing, she's in the wind. If the Russians find her before I do, you know that's not going to be pretty, and you brought her into whatever fuck-fest you have going on, so you better fucking help me find her."

There was a pause. Was he pumping his fist, or was he trying to figure a way to screw him? "Okay." He sounded as if he was walking. "I have limited resources. But let's meet up and figure the best way to track her down before anyone else does. The police are already out looking for her, and there have been some unconfirmed sightings of her in the Psiri district. Where are you? I can pick you up en route."

David was not down with that idea, but he had few choices with Molly in the wind. He cursed at her again. He would never let her forget this moronic move if they lived to be one hundred. If they lived. Jesus.

"Okay. Meet me at the corner of Sina and Skoufa," he said, coming up with the only place he knew the location of.

"Be there in thirty." Peterson hung up.

David deleted all his contacts, removed the memory card and slipped his phone into the pocket of a man at the bus stop as he walked past. He waited until the bus came and the man got on it before heading back toward the scenes of the crimes. As he rounded the corner, police sirens called out again, and he smiled as they rounded the corner and started following the bus. He hoped Molly had the sense to keep her battery separated from her phone as he'd asked her to.

He got to the restaurant that Victoria had invited them to—what was it, two days ago? Felt like a month ago.

He tried to piece together the pieces of a puzzle that had been worrying him. The inscription on the pen, "BP," which he was now sure didn't belong to Brandon Peterson. Having met him, he knew he was what he said he was, a low-level wonk—no way could he have rigged those explosives. The reporter covering the tri-cities. Peterson's girlfriend getting drunk and spilling the beans on an op. But what if she wasn't a US agent? What if she was a Russian agent recruited because Peterson was on the Russia desk? It wasn't that far of a stretch. He'd have to meet a lot of Russian companies and people. David also remembered the second SVR man telling him "*Spasibo*" in the temple. "Thank you" in Russian. And then he realized—ice shivered through his blood—BP, in the Russian alphabet, stands for VR in roman letters. Victoria Ruskin. She wasn't an agent, she was a full-blown SVR officer.

And then he hated himself. The last piece to the puzzle. The second shot at the cocktail party. Why shoot again if your target had been killed with your first shot? Unless your real target had crouched down to retrieve a dropped note?

He'd been so fucking stupid.

CHAPTER FIFTEEN

When Molly awoke, she was tied to a chair, with something nasty-tasting over her mouth. The side of her neck stung, possibly from the drug Victoria had given her. Victoria.

She struggled against her bonds, looking around the dimly lit room. No, it wasn't a room, it was more like a warehouse. She was tied to a chair in a freaking warehouse. Her brain shifted for a second as if she was watching a movie. She was in a movie. That was the only explanation for this level of craziness.

She blinked several times. Nope, she was still there. And she needed to pee like whoa. And nausea rolled in her stomach. She took a deep breath through her nose. Must not puke, must not puke. With tape over her mouth she'd probably drown in it. Her whole body was rejecting the scene in front of her, and she couldn't blame it at all. So Victoria was Russian? But she'd had such a normal accent. Nothing about her suggested she was anything other than what she'd said she was.

Molly wondered if she was a plant just to sit next to her on the plane, or if she was a real Russian spy who worked for a news show in America. But why was she wondering about Victoria when she should be wondering how she could get out of here alive?

She tried to see how she was tied to the chair. Looked like a mess of duct tape on her wrists and probably over her mouth. So why would they gag her if she was alone here? If they'd gagged her, there must be someone close who might overhear her.

There was a bang of metal on metal, and Victoria and the Russian man entered the warehouse from a door on the far side. It took them forever to walk to her, and in that time, her heart and stomach started pumping pure terror through her. She could feel herself shake, but she couldn't do anything about it.

Victoria ripped off the tape on her mouth. Her eyes were sad, somehow. Molly had been expecting some kind of viciousness that…well back to the movies again. In the movies, Victoria would have shot out a kneecap by now.

Why did her brain keep insisting that this was some kind of movie?

"I'm sorry, Molly. But you really should have come to the Media Club with me. We could have avoided all this."

"What? I don't understand," she rasped.

The Russian passed Victoria a bottle of water, who in turn held it to Molly's lips. As she sipped the water, she continued.

"It was a shame you got involved in our—I suppose you

could call it—our strategy for a new Europe." She crouched next to Molly.

"I can get you out of the country in a matter of hours, if you give me what Doubrov passed you."

Molly's heart raced. "I don't understand. He didn't pass me anything."

Victoria leaned in close to her ear and whispered. "I don't have time for this. This isn't a negotiation. You tell me, or you don't tell me. The latter would be no good for you."

"I'm telling you the truth. He didn't give me anything."

Her captor said nothing, just stood and turned her back to Molly. She spoke Russian to Mr. SVR who shrugged and walked back to the door through which they'd entered. It banged.

Victoria turned back to her, and Molly expected her to make some kind of plea. Some woman-to-woman request that would make Molly confess. But instead she just pricked her with a needle again, and before Molly could say anything, the world went black.

David scoped out the rendezvous point. First from the alleyway in which he and Molly had hidden from the Russian, and then from as many vantage points as he could manage, including from the roof. Peterson didn't seem to have sent an advance team. Maybe he could be trusted after all. God knew he needed someone he could trust right now. He needed to find Molly before Victoria found her.

He waited for Peterson, berating himself for not piecing this all together before now. She'd said her boyfriend was a policy wonk, and what the fuck "tri-cities" were there in DC? He'd been so stupid. So fucking slow. Jesus. If he couldn't get to Molly in time, he didn't know what he would do with himself. He figured his future at Barracks Security was over. He couldn't even trust himself to keep an innocent woman safe.

He stood with his back to the wall watching all ways at the small crossroads until he saw Peterson come into view and advance up toward the meeting point. He seemed nervous, checking behind him every few paces. David stepped forward to meet him.

Peterson acknowledged him with a slight nod.

Five steps. He'd taken five damn steps before Peterson's eyes widened and his pace stuttered.

Ice seeped into David's veins. He didn't need to look around to know he was about to be taken, and that Peterson probably knew nothing about it. He felt the heat of a large van behind him, and he knew he was too late to run, and clearly was at a disadvantage. A gun cocked.

Shit.

He held his hands out by his waist to minimize any tough-guy heroics these people might decide they need to perform. He took a breath and turned, hoping to see police as the lesser of two evils.

Nope. Three sets of eyes behind three balaclavas looked back at him from the sliding door of a van. Semiautomatic guns aimed at him. Yup. Nothing to see here. He turned back to Peterson, who was looking at his phone in disbelief.

Hands grabbed him and pulled him into the van. David went limp, hoping to keep from getting hurt in a way that might incapacitate him. As he was wondering if Molly was safe, and if he was at least being taken to her, a pinch at his neck filled him with warmth and tiredness.

"David. Wake up. *David*," a voice said, over and over. His shoulders hurt, not an unusual occurrence. His mouth burned as if he'd had really bad heartburn. Tasted terrible.

He tried to open his eyes, but couldn't manage to get them all the way open. And then he was lost in sleep again.

The next time he woke, a sharp pain ripped him from sleep. His shoulders felt like they were being ripped from his sockets.

"You like that?" a male voice asked.

Fuck. What was going on? David opened his eyes. He was in a warehouse, hanging from his hands. He twisted to see who was winching him up. He spun around on the chains. The Russian fucker. He was suspended so high that he could only touch the ground with his toes. And only if he got his shoes in the right position.

He'd been in this position exactly six years ago during his SERE training. He'd been captured, as they all had been, and subjected to questioning by the instructors. In that situation though, he knew they were supposed to hurt him, but not too badly, or with any lasting consequences. Just enough to make it real.

Not so much here.

He tried to kick out at the tall man, but he easily avoided David's attempt. All the KGB guy did was nod over to the corner.

He spun around again. Molly. His heart clenched.

"What did you do to her?" he growled. She was tied to a chair with some kind of tape, head lolling to one side as if she was asleep. He forced his brain not to consider the possibility that she might be dead. But his heart went there anyway. It was as if his heart was being gripped and wrenched out of his body. Pure anger and frustration poured out of him in a howl of rage.

Before he could test his binds, Molly roused, unfocused and bleary-eyed. "What? Who's there?" She shook her head several times as if to clear her vision. "What…? David?" She moaned. "I thought it was a dream. I wanted so much for it to have been a dream."

Relief spiked through him, bringing a calming influence on his body. He still wanted to fucking rip that guy's head off. Fucking Russians. But at least Molly was alive.

The man in the gray suit popped his cuffs and rolled his neck. "I'm going to leave you two to get reacquainted." He sauntered to the door as if he didn't have a care in the world. He probably didn't.

"Are you okay? What happened?" David tried to see if she'd been harmed. He couldn't see anything obvious.

"I'm fine. They just keep sedating me with something. I don't know what it is. One prick and I'm out of it. Are you hurt?" Her voice sounded normal but tense.

"I'm fine," he said, trying for his own normal voice. "Just, you know, hanging around."

She choked a laugh, and then reprimanded him. "That's not funny."

"Sorry. How did you get here?" He wasn't going to mention

her escape, he didn't want to remind her that she didn't trust him…because trussed up like a dead cow on a hook, he probably didn't instill trust now either.

"Victoria. My reporter friend? She offered me an escape route when the police were closing in on me, and when I opened the car door, he was holding a gun on me." She nodded toward the door he'd disappeared through. "Are you really all right? You look like hell."

He shrugged and then winced. "My shoulders is all," he said, trying to position himself on his toes to relieve some of the strain.

"This is bad isn't it? They can't let us go now. Victoria has basically outed herself as a Russian…what? An agent? Collaborator?"

"I suspect she's an SVR operative, like the suit. Probably deep undercover. She'll either have to go back to Russia, or yes, eliminate anyone who knows who she is." There was no point sugarcoating it. "But I'm going to get us out of here. So don't worry about that."

Her expression was blank, and he suddenly saw what she saw. A helpless washout, hanging from a meathook in a disused warehouse. How could she possibly have faith in him?

He hoped he could prove her—and maybe himself—wrong.

Hoped.

"I'm so sorry to get you involved in this, David," she said. "This is all my fault." She couldn't even look at him.

"It's not your fault, it's Peterson's fault. And the fucking Russians' fault. But don't worry, we're going to take the whole outfit down when we get out of here." He hoped he sounded confident, but the frown didn't fall from her face, so probably he didn't manage to convince her.

The door slammed again, but he didn't have the energy to spin around and lose his tenuous grip on the floor with the toe of his shoes.

He looked inquisitively at Molly who mouthed "Victoria" at him.

"You're both awake. That's great," she said in her perfect East Coast accent.

David wondered how long she'd been undercover. He wasn't going to say anything unless pressed. Chatty Cathies never won the day. Made it too easy for their captors to get what they wanted.

"So," she continued, as if they were all at some kind of cocktail party. "My people tell me that Doubrov passed you something before he was shot." She paused for a second as if collecting her thoughts. "He asked to see you, didn't he?"

Molly started, and David went still. Doubrov asked to see Molly? She hadn't told him that. A bad feeling wafted through the warehouse like an unwelcome draft. What else hadn't she told him?

Victoria noticed her response. "I see I am right." She also seemed surprised. Molly needed to learn a poker face or she was going to give Victoria everything she needed.

"I'm not telling you anything," Molly said. Her voice wavered but her gaze didn't. She was one hell of a woman. He looked around for something to use as leverage. Anything that would get him free.

"You have to, sweetie. We don't have much time. If you tell me what I need to know, I'm going to let you go. Leave you here, obviously, but you'll be free eventually. I think the warehouse workers start work at seven a.m. on Monday.

David shook his head at Molly from behind Victoria's head. *Don't believe her.* It was a convincing effort from Victoria. Hardship, pain, starvation, but no death. It sounded plausible, but he didn't believe her for a moment. He willed Molly not to fall for it. But in all honesty, half of him wanted to know what she knew too. Obviously she'd been keeping things from him too. More evidence that she didn't trust him. Okay. He steeled himself. He probably couldn't ever persuade her that she could trust him. But he could persuade *himself* that he was trustworthy.

The only thing he knew was that if the Russians wanted information, he wasn't going to give it to them. Wait, what had she said? *Time was running out?* That didn't sound good. Not good at all. There had to be a larger picture. The big operation that Russia was planning at the G20 meeting? Had to be something huge. Devastating.

David ran through everything he knew. Victoria becomes Peterson's girlfriend to get the in on the DOS end of their diplomacy. Maybe she gets drunk, and says enough to tip Peterson off. Peterson taps Molly to pass Doubrov a note warning him that the Russian finance minister was going to be taken. But by whom? Why? It all sounded too Cold War to be plausible.

The engraving on the pen that had been used as the connection point of the improvised explosive. Victoria was the hardcore operative he and Mal had discussed. She'd killed Doubrov...His mind stuttered. He remembered what he'd been thinking about when he'd been drugged. The second shot. The first shot had taken Doubrov out, but only because Molly had bent down to pick up the note.

Molly had been the target. Victoria had been trying to kill Molly.

Jesus, the pain was really focusing his mind. "Don't tell her anything, Mol. She's the one who tried to kill you, but got Doubrov instead." He needed to get Victoria's attention on him.

"Did you get into trouble when you accidentally killed Doubrov instead of Molly? Are you tying up loose ends by killing us both? Will you also kill Peterson? Your boyfriend? You want to know how I knew it was you? You used your own monogrammed pen as your trip-wire contact blocker."

It worked. She snapped open a baton and wacked him across his stretched ribs. His feet gave way and he swung, the pain humming though him like the echo of a choirboy's last note.

"That wasn't my fault. I had to improvise. My target spotter couldn't spot his own ass in a mirror. I know who you are, Sergeant David Church. Explosive Ordinance Disposal. If it had been anyone but you, my bombs would have gone off as planned and none of this would have happened. It's all your fault. It's all your fault." She punctuated each word with a lash of her baton.

He grit his teeth and shouted through them, not giving her the satisfaction of seeing him groan or fucking whimper in pain, which is what he wanted to do. SERE training. Don't give the enemy the psychological advantage. If you're scared, in pain, or weak, act angry.

"Don't!" Molly said. "I'll tell you anything you want. Just don't hurt him. He didn't have anything to do with this. I just met him here. I'm the one you need to talk to. Although I'm afraid it's too late for you."

David's head snapped up. What the fuck was she talking about? Victoria's attention was one hundred percent on Molly now. He looked up at the binds around his wrists that were attached to the chain. When she'd hit him and he'd weighed down on them, he'd felt them rip a bit.

"I knew you weren't just the innocent bystander my boss thought you were," Victoria said, leaning in satisfaction against a wooden table and folding her arms across her pink jacket. "Tell me more."

"I want some water first. For me and David. Then I'll talk," Molly said, coughing for effect.

Victoria screwed her face up for a second, and then shrugged. "Okay. But if you don't talk…what am I saying? Of course you'll talk. You really have no choice."

She made the long walk to the door of the warehouse and slipped out. "What are you doing? She will kill you once you've given her what she wants. It was you she was after in the first place." His heart was racing at the little time they had.

"I know. I just don't want you here when that happens. I dragged you into this, and I'm so sorry. I had no idea this would get so…"

"Fucked up?" he asked between his teeth.

"Yeah. I'm going to give her enough information to let you go. Then, I guess, we'll see what happens." She was numb. She knew she should be petrified, but she couldn't gather enough emotion to feel anything. Every part of her wanted him away from this. She had no idea how seeing her die would affect him, but given the last year, she had her suspicions. If she could just save him from this, she would be okay. She would die with no regrets. Well, that wasn't really true, but she was trying her hardest to hold it all together.

"You're sweet," he said. "But you really don't have to do that for me." Suddenly there was no strain in his voice at all. It was like they were having coffee somewhere. "Just shuffle yourself over here a bit."

She used her body to jump her chair over to David.

"Sorry about this," he said as he put his feet on her thighs. He was using the extra height to try to flip his chains off the hook hanging from the ceiling. "I need more height."

Crap. She used all her energy to shuffle over to the big wooden table that Victoria had put her case on. When she'd laid it there, Molly imagined it was full of torture devices.

"We have to hurry, sweetheart." Still his voice held no tension.

She pushed the back of her chair against the table and shoved it. The effort was wearing her out. She felt weak and she didn't know if it was from the drug they'd kept giving her, or the fact that she'd been strapped to the chair for…how long she didn't really know. She pushed, and shoved. Willing herself to find the energy to move the table to him.

"Just a bit further, you're doing great." As he said the words, the door slammed open.

Shit. She gave one more shove, mustering all the energy she could. The momentum moved the table about a foot or two, and left Molly hanging in midair for a second before she crashed to the ground. She rolled on to her side to get her eyes on David.

From her prone position, she saw Victoria's legs running toward them, but couldn't see David's legs, which hopefully meant that he was on the table. A crash of chains echoed around the room. Molly took a breath and tried to figure out how she could help him.

She rolled to try to get some leverage and heard the chair creaking. Maybe she could break it. She was sure she'd seen Black Widow do this in a movie. She rolled against the back of the chair. There was a snap as one of the chair arms detached from the back. Nice.

She rolled harder, slamming the chair against the concrete. Pain radiated through her bones as the back splintered away from the arms. She heard grunts, and the rattle of chains. Frantically she beat her bent legs down hard. Again and again, trying not to notice the shots of pain that radiated through her. One last crash, and the legs of the chair had broken. They were still attached to her, but they'd broken off the seat.

She leapt up. David was standing, barely. He was slumped as if he couldn't stand up anymore. Victoria lay on the floor, one of her legs pointing in a very unnatural direction, unconscious. Maybe dead.

She got to David just in time to put her hands on him before he fell to the ground. She managed to brace his fall. "You were awesome," she said. "You saved us." She kissed the side of his head and held him, doing little more than rocking in relief. Her brain went fuzzy, and she closed her eyes, just wanting to be anywhere but here.

She roused herself to untie David's wrists, and then her own when David just groaned. "We have to go. Can you stand?" she asked. The fight must have really taken it out of him. She pulled herself to her feet leaning on the table. She leaned down to pull David up, and for the first time, saw blood on the floor. Sticky dark blood. A pool.

She sank to her knees. "David? Are you hurt?" She tried to check him, but it wasn't until she held him that she realized he was bleeding from his side.

"Go, sweetheart. They want *you*. You have to run. Go to the embassy. Ask them to call Sadie Walker. She's a friend of Harry and Matt's. Tell her everything. Everything you haven't told me. She's…" his voice faded.

"Fuck that all to hell. I'm not leaving here without you." Suddenly immune to her own injuries, she looked around for something to help him.

Victoria's case. She opened it. Torture devices? It was the suitcase she'd arrived with. Just freaking clothes, a wallet and…an iPad. She frantically rifled through her wallet and plucked out a credit card and pressed it against his wound to make the gaping hole airtight. She grabbed one of Victoria's silk shirts and wrapped it around him, tying the arms around his waist to hold it in place.

He was barely conscious now, and as adrenaline pumped

through her she knew she needed to get him away from the warehouse before the Russian came back with the water Victoria had requested. Otherwise David wouldn't get the help he needed.

She was about to lift David on to his feet, when her brain registered a ringing sound. "Can you stand?" she asked. He waved his hand at her, in what would be a convincing shoo-away if it hadn't been for the table he was leaning against scraping back on the concrete floor.

Victoria stirred at the sound of the phone, but didn't come to. Thank God. Molly wasn't sure if she could knock her out, although she was fairly certain she could outrun her. She made sure David was upright and likely to stay that way for a second, and went back to Victoria's things. Phone. She had a phone. Where the hell was it?

She looked through the whole bag, and then started on the zipper pockets. There. Front pocket, along with a gun. She took the phone and left the gun.

A car door slammed outside, and without hesitating she went for the gun, tucked it into David's back pocket, and wrapped his arm around her shoulders. "Gotta walk now, okay? Come on."

She half dragged him to the opposite side of the warehouse, behind some large wooden crates, to a window. Shit. There was water out there. She sat David down on the concrete, "Shhh." She laid her fingers across his mouth and felt him nod beneath her hand.

She took the phone and dialed the only number she knew by heart. Her boss's—Harry's.

Harry picked up the phone immediately. "Hello?"

"Harry, it's me," she whispered.

"Who? I can't hear."

Molly looked at the phone. It had all the bars.

"Molly," she ground out, peeking through the crates. The Russian was in the building now. And the whole place suddenly seemed like one big echo chamber. She hung up the phone, and texted Harry instead.

It's Molly. Kidnapped by Russians with David Church in warehouse by the sea in Athens.

God, she hoped they were still in Athens.

He's injured, but told me to get Sadie Walker on it?

She waited for a reply, and then realized that the text notifying ring would echo all around the warehouse basically identifying where they were. She fumbled for the settings, but it was too late.

Shit. She stuffed the phone into her pocket without reading the reply and looked for somewhere to run. She considered pushing David out of the window, but worried that he wouldn't be able to stay afloat without her there. They sat in silence as the minutes ticked by. She was worried if she waited much longer to make a decision he'd bleed out in front of her.

She made her decision. She would leave David there, and give the Russian what he wanted, and try to buy some time. She held her hands up and stepped out from behind the row of shipping crates.

What?

The Russian was gone.

So was Victoria, and the broken chair, and her suitcase. It

was like nothing had happened there. Even the pool of David's blood had gone. Had she imagined the whole thing?

A noise came from behind her, she turned to find David, holding a gun out, leaning against one of the crates.

"They've gone," she said.

He slumped, and she ran the few short paces to his side and slipped his arm around her shoulders again. "Come on. Let's get out of here."

It took forever to cross the warehouse with David barely able to stumble, let alone walk. Every step that echoed around the building worried Molly that someone would come out of the shadows and kill them. She didn't care so much about herself, but she needed to get David to safety. Get him a doctor.

After about ten minutes, her own legs started wobbling under both their weight. She was sweating hard. She hoped it was a side effect of the drug she'd been jabbed with, but the exertion was killing her. At least that's how it felt. She was cold, sweaty and shaky. Just a few more steps to get out.

Just a few more steps.

Just a few…

She reached for the door handle, but it was farther away than she thought.

A few more steps. Her fingertips scraped the metal of the door. She pulled it open with the rest of her energy.

Daylight.

And the metal-on-metal cocking of a lot of weapons.

"Hold it."

"Hands up!"

"Show me your hands."

She slumped to the ground, her last action was to try to make sure David fell on her, and not the hard ground. He did.

She didn't care about the guns. Relief was the last emotion her consciousness registered.

They had American accents.

CHAPTER SIXTEEN

She came to in the back of an ambulance. The only other occupants were a paramedic and a woman in a HELLO KITTY T-shirt. Molly had an oxygen mask over her face and a drip in her arm.

"Where's David?" she asked, her voice muffled by the mask.

Hello Kitty looked at the paramedic, who nodded and lowered the mask.

"I'm sorry, honey?"

"Where's David?" Molly noticed there were straps holding her to the bed. She struggled against them, trying to understand what was going on.

Hello Kitty undid one of the restraining bands. "You're not a prisoner. We're transporting you to the medical center at the embassy. I'm Sadie. Harry's friend."

Molly wanted to feel fear, or hope, or relief, but there was no emotion inside her. Like at all.

"I know you're feeling strange, but that's the chemical we're giving you to combat the drug that you had in your system. We don't know what it is, so we're giving you a generic drug that will counter the effects of most sedatives. The only side effect is that you'll feel weird for a while. It's artificially equalizing all the hormones and chemicals inside you.

Molly nodded. "Sadie?"

"I'm glad I found you. I think Harry might have killed me if I hadn't." She gave a rueful smile. "Is there anything you can tell me about what happened to you?"

Molly told her what had happened to her since the assassination.

"We can't find any evidence of the kidnapping in the warehouse, Molly. I'm sorry. So that means we don't have anything actionable to take to the Russians. Or to the United Nations. It's just a wash right now." Sadie stared out of the side window, with a frown.

And then she realized that Sadie hadn't told her what had happened to David. Her brain knew that was wrong. Something was wrong. But her body couldn't process the feeling. Well her brain was going to have to do the job of her heart too. "Where's David?"

Sadie looked at her watch. "I'm waiting for an update. He'd lost a lot of blood, I'm afraid. But they're doing their best. Harry and Matt told me he was a strong guy. We're just hoping he's strong enough. You did a good job with the credit card and the bandage, by the way." She smiled and checked her watch again.

"The credit card," Molly said. "I took it from Victoria

Ruskin's purse. There must be some way you can trace her with that?"

Sadie held her gaze for a moment. "We also have the gun that was in David's possession. With the credit card, maybe eventually we'll be able to make something stick. But it's not much.

Molly made a decision. "If you take me to David, I'll give you two other things that might help you. One thing I'll give you now. The other thing, later."

She handed Sadie the notes that had started everything.

Molly sat by David's bed. There was no freaking way she was going to let him walk away from her again. Mission or no mission. Injury or no injury. As long as she had eyes on him she felt…nothing. *Dammit.* Enough with this antidote or whatever it was.

She traced the tube of the IV attached to her wheelchair and found the plastic tap, and turned it off. Then she took out the needle from the back of her hand. It hurt. On TV, the tough guys yank it out like it's nothing, but it hurt like hell. Turns out nothing is really like it is on television.

Her eyes flickered to the small screen attached to the wall in the corner of the room. No one was talking about the assassination anymore. A scientist had conclusively—he said—proved that fracking will kill the planet's infrastructure within fifty years. So that had been the main headline since she'd got to the hospital. Some people believed him, some didn't. So she suspected after all the furor, things would go back to normal. But meantime, the 3D hologram of the collapse of the planet that he'd shown at his presentation was on every channel. She watched the implosion on the TV for about the tenth time.

"Is the world ending?" A hoarse voice came from the bed.

"David!"

"So that's a yes?" he said, trying to reach for a glass of water.

"Stop! Don't...pull anything. You have more stitches than the curtains there. Just let me bring it to you. She struggled with her wheelchair for a second, and smiled at her own attempts to get out without putting the brake on.

"Jesus. Why are you in that wheelchair? What happened?" He winced as he tried to move.

"Don't do that either. Let me adjust the bed so you can see that I'm fine. They put me in it because of the drugs Victoria gave me. A lot, apparently."

She sat on the bed and held the water to his lips. He sipped and cleared his throat.

"They didn't take you out of the country?" he asked, concern etched across his face.

Molly looked down at the bed. "They wanted to, but I made a deal with them to stay."

"And why would you have done that?" He frowned.

"I wanted to make sure you didn't die. But now I know you're okay, I'll be off. Nice knowing you..." She got up to leave, brushing imaginary lint from her jeans.

"I don't blame you, sweetheart. I let you down back there. I'm so..."

"What? Are you kidding me? You never let me down. Not once." She was taken aback that he'd thought that for a moment.

He frowned again. "You left. I figured you'd had enough of me leading you into danger," he half choked out, half whispered.

Her stomach contorted at the thought that he'd been carrying this. "Oh my God. I'm so sorry. It never occurred to me that you'd think that. I left because I hated myself that I'd got you involved in the mess I was in. I just wanted you to have…what do they call it? Plausible deniability? I didn't want you to go to jail for helping me. I wanted you safe. You'd already been through so much…that was all it was." Tears leaked out of her eyes as she stood up.

He grabbed her hand. "Not so fast, sweetheart. I'm not letting anyone debrief you except me. Last time you were debriefed we all ended up here. What happened to Peterson, by the way?"

"Being raked over the coals by the embassy staff, I heard," Molly said. "Anyway, before I make up my mind to stay or go…what kind of debriefing did you have in mind? Because, I should tell you now. I'm not wearing any."

"I'm planning on debriefing you for a long, long time. Just…as soon as I can move without morphine."

Joy flooded her veins with such power that tears started falling. "I'm sorry, it's not you, it's the drug." She swiped at her tears and held tissues to her nose. She wasn't really sure that was true.

"It had better be me." He pressed the button on his remote control, and slowly, very, very slowly, the bed slid upright, so his lips were inches away from hers.

"I guess…it was always you," she breathed, as she leaned forward to claim her future.

EPILOGUE

David checked into the hotel again, this time under a fake name, getting an uncomfortable feeling of déjà vu. The receptionist handed him a key and a letter, sealed in an envelope. He extended the handle of his suitcase and headed toward the elevator. Once away from the desk, he opened the letter.

A grin spread across his face, and a tiny sliver of unease. He hoped she wasn't going to do to him what he'd done to her the year before. He looked around the lobby and spotted her, ostensibly reading an Athens newspaper upside-down while waiting in line for the receptionist. He tried not to laugh. He leaned against the pillar where he had checked his email on his phone that morning after the cocktail party. Whatever happened to Mal? He couldn't wait to find out what mess he'd gotten himself into. Bound to be a good story. All he knew was that Baston was furious with him. So that warmed the cockles.

"I simply must have the same room I was in before. I loved it so much. You understand. A girl wants what a girl wants. Can you see if it's available? It was number 1214? I'm only staying for the one night." He could hear Molly chatting up the receptionist from where he was. She played the demanding guest to a T.

She was also quite demanding with him too. Thinking about the *unique* physical therapy she'd been threatening him with had sped up his healing to no end. And today was the first day they'd been able to finish the mission. The leadership conference started in ten days, and the hotel was emptying out in preparation. They already knew that room 1214 was empty now.

"Thank you *so* much," Molly said, as she pulled her suitcase toward the elevators. He joined her, and they stared at the elevator doors pretending not to know each other. They stepped back as other guests got off the elevator, and then got on. Just as the doors were about to close, a hand snaked around them, making them open again.

Sadie. "If you think I trust you two alone in a hotel room while I'm waiting patiently downstairs, you're very mistaken.

David didn't reply, but Molly giggled. He still couldn't believe she'd kept this secret from him, and from Victoria. But he would exact his punishment. Again, and again.

They all got off on the twelfth floor, and Molly led the way to the room. She opened the door, and David and Sadie followed.

"Okay. Wait here," Molly said. She went into the bathroom and stood on the side of the bath. David shook his head in disbelief as they both watched her through the doorway. How would an archaeologist come up with this shit?

She popped a ceiling tile and felt around. An expression of victory lit up her lovely face. "Got it!"

She handed it over with a solemn, "Use this only for good," and Sadie took it, rolling her eyes. They all looked at it in her palm. It was a key with a website address scratched on its leather fob.

"Doubrov slipped it to me as soon as he saw me. I don't think he had any idea that I was also trying to slip him something, which is why he froze. I guess we both did. I didn't know what it was, so I hid it in the bathroom. I didn't mention it, because I didn't know who I could trust." Molly looked at David. "I do now."

"I'll give it to the station director and see if he can figure out what it is." Sadie said, tucking it into her pocket. "It was nice meeting you both, but remember what you signed. You can't talk about what happened here to anyone. Not about Doubrov, the key, the note…and especially about me. Clear?"

"Absolutely," Molly said.

"Crystal." David replied. He'd signed so many of those documents during his time in the military that he barely even thought about it.

"Good luck to you," Sadie said to David, as she opened the door. "You might need to handcuff her to something to keep her out of trouble. You know what to do now." The door slammed and she was gone.

"She has good ideas, that woman," David said taking out a cotton handkerchief.

"What? What do you know what to do?" Molly said, hand on hips.

"You in handcuffs." He started to wipe down every surface they had touched. The bathroom door, the wall that Molly had braced herself against to climb up to the ceiling, and the ceiling tile itself, not that it held fingerprints well, but you couldn't be too careful. "Now let's go, and we can talk about how Doubrov gave you something that you failed to tell me about." He basically knew what had happened, but he wanted her to admit that she'd done it to keep him safe. Crazy, stupid, amazing woman.

He nodded her toward the door, wiping down everything she touched, until they were outside the door. He grabbed her hand and led her down the corridor and around the corner to room 1256, which he'd been given.

The door had barely closed before he told her to strip.

"What? No foreplay?" She quirked a coquettish eyebrow at him before kicking off one shoe and then the other.

"I just need to know that the archaeologist-spy isn't hiding anything else from me." He pulled out the desk chair and sat, unwilling to admit that he was tired. "Everything. Maybe you're wearing a wire?"

She started to unbutton her blouse, unable to hide a grin. "I've given all that up. I'm never accepting a meeting from a government official ever again. It's hazardous to my health."

"Good. I'm happy to hear you've learned your lesson.

She dropped her blouse, revealing a lilac bra, the lace of which only barely covered her nipples, and her skirt, which she was already unzipping. His dick hardened at the sight of her, as it did annoyingly often. The skirt also fell to the floor.

She was wearing matching tiny, lilac lace shorts and hold-up stockings. Holding her arms up and slowly turning, she said, "See? No wires. Is there anything else you'd like to check me for?"

"Take the rest of it off." He tried to keep his face stern, and it wasn't too much of a challenge, because the box in his pocket was poking at his stitches. "Come on, quickly. I have something I want you to wear for me."

"Oh, exciting," she said, eyeing his suitcase. "What did you bring?"

He looked meaningfully at her and folded his arms across his chest.

She moved closer to him so that their knees touched. She unhooked her bra at the front, and let her lush breasts go free. She bent over slightly, and he couldn't stop himself from stroking her soft skin. She let him touch her for a couple of seconds, and then shimmied away a few inches. She turned around, bending at the waist as she took her panties off. As she did, his eyes didn't leave her lush ass. As she swept down her stockings, he could see all of her. He stroked her ass and felt her pussy. She shivered and moved back closer to him. This had gotten totally off topic, but he couldn't resist her wetness and the whimper that came from her throat as he touched her clit.

His dick strained against his pants, and reminded him of his own mission. Pulling her onto his lap, he brought her head down so that he could kiss her.

"What did you bring for me to wear?" she asked, breathless.

He produced the box and flipped it open with one hand. Sadie had helped him choose the ring.

"What?" she said eyes wide and disbelieving.

"I know it's sudden, and I won't want us to rush into anything. But I want you in my life forever. And I don't want you to ever think that I won't come back for you. But if you wear this, it also means that you have to come back to me too. We're both going to be traveling a lot with our jobs, and this is my promise to you that when you're ready, we'll put down roots somewhere and spend the rest of our lives together. Will you wear it?"

Tears spilled from her eyes. "Yes. Yes of course. And you better always come for me. And you better not leave me for a year." She narrowed her watery eyes at him.

"No more than a week or so, ever again." He slipped the ring on her finger and as it reached its resting place, he said, "maybe no more than a few days." He stroked her thigh. "Maybe no more than a few hours."

She leaned in. "That sounds about right." Her lips touched his, and he lost himself in her once again.

Please turn the page for a look at the first book in Emmy Curtis's sinfully sexy military romance Alpha Ops series,

OVER THE LINE.

Chapter One

Khost Province, Afghanistan

Alone at last," Walker whispered as he crouched next to Beth. Dust flew up as the crack of a bullet hitting the ground ricocheted around the valley. He flattened himself next to her.

"You are *shit* at taking orders," she hissed back.

He ignored her as he tried to figure out where the shots were coming from. If he could just neutralize the immediate threat, he could patch her up and get her to safety. His blood had flashed ice-cold when she radioed that she'd been hit. And she'd still been laying down covering fire for the guys when he'd found her. If she was the first taste of females in combat, bring it on.

A pool of dark blood glistened in the hazy moonlight, expanding and trickling across the sand as he watched.

Crap.

Their simple mission of relieving another patrol group had gone to hell in a handbasket. Another shot echoed around them, and this time Walker was ready to identify the telltale muzzle flash. As soon as he saw it, he swung his gun and sent a shot downrange toward the insurgent.

Silence. He took that as a good sign.

"Okay, Sergeant. Turn over so I can look at that leg."

Beth grunted but complied, biting back a moan as she did.

Walker's heart dropped when he saw that her BDU pants were completely soaked with blood. A lot of it. *Shit.* Maybe the bullet had nicked an artery. He grabbed his knife and cut away the pant leg to expose the wound. It was about two inches below her panty line. And blood was still pumping out in rhythm with her heartbeat.

He undid her belt and pulled it off. No way was he going to let her die in this crappy valley, in the middle of Shithole City, Bumfuck. No fucking way.

As he slid the belt around the top of her thigh, trying not to touch anything that could get him court-martialed, one of the Strike Eagles he had called for screamed overhead. He threw himself over Beth, and waited for the bombs to drop.

They exploded with precision, of course. Walker had been the one to give them the coordinates. That was his job. The only air force guy on the team, he was the one who communicated with the aircraft patrolling the skies above the war zone. The only one who could give the bombers precise targets. The valley lit up with orange fire as they detonated. Rocks and scree sprinkled them, sounding like heavy rain, feeling like stones.

That should keep the Taliban out of his hair for a bit. He

made to get up and realized how close to Beth's face his was. He hesitated for a split second. A bad, bad second. He'd been deployed with her unit for a couple of months and had spent most of the time dreaming about her at night, and trying to ignore those dreams by day.

He swallowed, and went back to business. "I have to tourniquet your leg. It's going to hurt like a fucker," he said as he fastened the belt as high on her thigh as he could manage. "Just think, all this time I wanted to see your panties, and finally…"

Beth opened her mouth, probably to give him hell, and he used the distraction to pull the belt tight.

"You bastard," she ground out between gritted teeth.

The wound stopped pumping blood and he silently thanked whoever was looking out for them upstairs. He grabbed the first-aid kit from his pack and took out gauze and dark green bandages. A shot sounded again, and sand flew up just inches away from his foot.

Shit.

Walker threw himself down again, this time lying between her legs, face about five inches from her wound. Which meant it was seven inches from her…

"Well, this is awkward," he murmured. It worked, and in relief he heard her gasp a laugh.

"Next time…buy me dinner…first, all right?" she said between pants of Lamaze-type breathing.

He laughed quietly. "I've got to get you out of here first. Then I promise I will." He loosened the tourniquet, and watched to see if the blood flow had stopped. It hadn't, but it wasn't pumping out as it had been before. He tightened it and vowed not to check again.

"Walker," she ground out. "I have a letter. It's in my pants pocket." She groaned as if she was trying to get control over the pain. "Take it out before it gets soaked in blood. Make sure my sister gets it if I...don't make it."

He didn't waste time placating her; he stuffed his hand into her thigh pocket and grabbed the papers in there. He found the letter and stuffed it in his own pocket, before replacing the notebook and loose papers back in hers. "Got it. I'll look after it. But I'm going to do everything I can to get you home to her, okay?"

"Look!" Beth grimaced as she propped herself up on one elbow and pointed up the valley where they had left their truck. A huge cloud of sand was making its way toward them, seemingly in slow motion. She made as if to get up, but fell back down with a moan as soon as she tried her leg.

The impending sandstorm made up his mind. They couldn't get stuck in it—Beth would die in all likelihood. If they didn't move now, the storm would be on them, and no rescue would be able to get to them until it dissipated. No time for second-guessing.

A cloud passed in front of the moon, and Walker instinctively jumped up. "Put your weight on your good leg." He held her opposite hand as if they were about to shake hands, and he pulled her up. "Come on, Garcia. Walk it off."

She breathed a laugh as he bent his knees and gently slid her over his shoulder in a fireman's carry, so her good leg bore the brunt of pressure against his shoulder. She wriggled pretty weakly in protest.

"What the fuck? Put me down. I can walk," she said, her words not reflected by the strain in her voice.

Yeah, not so much. "Sure you can, sweetheart…I mean Sergeant. But we need to run. Are you going to stay with me?"

"I've got your six," she whispered.

He launched his pack on his other shoulder and took off, away from the sandstorm. He knew he could outrun it—it was slow-moving—but the quicker he could get her to a reasonable landing zone, the quicker the helicopters would land and get her to a hospital.

The cloud passed the moon and in the sudden light they were sitting ducks. Another shot rang out, whizzing past so close he could feel it rip the air next to his face. Beth's stomach tensed muscles against his shoulder and she pulled herself up. One hell of a soldier. One hell of a woman.

She let off three shots as he ran, and then she flopped back down. "Got him," she said. And then there was silence except for his own breathing that filled his head. Blood pounded in his ears as he ran. Blood pumping, and breath puffing.

In out, in out, nearly there, nearly there.

His muscles strained under her weight, and the eighty pounds of their combined body armor, but he'd trained for this, and frankly, it wasn't his first rodeo. It was his eighth. His legs kept pumping toward safety.

He hoped.

The familiar *whop whop* of a helicopter penetrated his thoughts, as well as the more constant gunshots as he neared the last of their vehicles. Five soldiers were on the ground, firing their weapons into the hills opposite them.

He skidded to a halt and laid Beth down. He dropped alongside her and asked for a sit rep from the guys.

"Marks took one to the face. We lost him. There seem to be about eight TBs left in the hillside, but they're not giving up. Only small arms fired, so I figured the helo can land over there to the right of the valley entrance." The soldier pointed to the only real possible landing zone for the choppers.

"I have to go clear the LZ, Beth. I'll be back." He looked at her but she didn't look back. Eyes closed and barely breathing, she looked like she had already checked out. His heart clenched.

No. Fucking. Way. He pulled the tourniquet tight again, and started CPR. "Hey, you." He slapped the nearest soldier on his helmet. "I need you to do CPR while I clear the landing zone, okay? Keep the tourniquet tight."

The soldier took over without question. And then realized who it was. "Shit, is this Garcia? Oh man, my wife will kill me if I let her die," he said.

"So will I. Keep that thought in the very front of your mind. I'll be back in a few." He hesitated for a second. Could he trust the soldier with her? Everything in him wanted to stay and breathe life into her himself, but he was the only one who could talk the pararescuers in, and the only one who could clear a landing zone to the pilots' satisfaction.

Walker grabbed his radio and one of the soldiers' flashlights, and ran to the potential LZ. He walked the square, checking for IEDs or anything suspicious. He didn't think there would be, because the convoy had passed over this area on their way into the valley. He could still see their tire tracks.

But it was better to be safe than sorry. As he paced, he couldn't stop thinking about Beth. How pale and lifeless she looked in the moonlight, how shallow her breathing, and how totally opposite that was to how she normally was: vibrant, prickly, beautiful, and strong.

The gentle *whop whop* of the helicopters became much louder as he finalized checking the LZ. He took out his radio.

"This is Playboy. PJs come in."

There were a few seconds of silence, during which he checked his radio for loose wires. Then, "This is PJ one, Playboy. How're we looking?"

"We have five able soldiers, one KIA, and one seriously injured. I've set up the landing zone at these coordinates." He rattled off a series of numbers.

"Can you light it up?"

"Roger that." Walker snapped some green chem lights from his pocket, and threw them to the corners of the cleared landing zone. He would normally use flares, but he didn't want to give the Taliban an invitation to pick the PJs as their new target. Once it was clear the helo was good to land, he sprinted back to Beth. *Please, God. I'll do anything if you just let me get her to the hospital alive.*

The second trail helicopter opened fire into the hills, backing up the guys on the ground. Two Combat Rescue Officers ran from the helicopter toward them, weapons drawn. They took one look at Beth and started work on her. They secured her tourniquet and put an oxygen mask over her face.

Walker stood back and let them run with her back to the helo. His heart rate finally normalized, but the clenched fist in his stomach did not fade. Following the others to safety, all he could see was Beth's white face, and he wondered if she would live to have the promised dinner with him. As he unclenched his fists to climb into the Pave Hawk helo, he realized his fingers were crossed.

Read Simon and Sadie's story in
COMPROMISED, coming Spring 2016!